Now...a
Harlequin
romance
by Anne Mather
comes to life
on the movie screen

starring
KEIR DULLEA · SUSAN PENHALIGON

Leopard in the Snow

Guest Stars
KENNETH MORE · BILLIE WHITELAW

featuring GORDON THOMSON as MICHAEL
and JEREMY KEMP as BOLT

Produced by JOHN QUESTED and CHRIS HARROP
Screenplay by ANNE MATHER and JILL HYEM
Directed by GERRY O'HARA

An Anglo-Canadian Co-Production

Other titles by

JANET DAILEY
IN HARLEQUIN PRESENTS

JANET DAILEY

reilly's woman

Harlequin Books

TORONTO • LONDON • NEW YORK • AMSTERDAM • SYDNEY

Harlequin Presents edition published April 1978
ISBN 0-373-70731-2

Original hardcover edition published in 1977
by Mills & Boon Limited

CHAPTER ONE

The pages of the magazine were flipped with an impatient finger. The articles couldn't hold Leah Talbot's attention as she kept glancing at the clock on the wall above the reception desk.

Outside, the gold ball of the sun was dipping closer to the horizon. Its light cast a pale yellow hue on the wings of the small planes parked on the hangar apron outside.

The clatter of the typewriter stopped. The dark-haired woman behind the reception desk rose from her chair, turning to her co-worker, an older woman with light hair that had been rinsed to a brassy shade to conceal the gray.

"Want a cup of coffee, June?" the dark-haired woman inquired. The older woman nodded without glancing from the account books spread across her desk. With two cups in hand, the brunette walked to the waist-high counter door, deftly swinging it open with her hip.

She smiled politely at Leah. "How about you, Miss Talbot? Would you like a refill?"

Glancing at the empty styrofoam cup sitting on the table in front of her, Leah hesitated, then shrugged, "Why not?" A faintly cynical grimace touched her sensually curved mouth.

Absently Leah smoothed the lightweight material of her camel tan skirt as she picked up her cup and, sidestepping her luggage, followed the woman.

"Getting tired of waiting?" The woman's question was rhetorical and sympathetic.

Breathing in deeply, Leah carried the thought further. "And getting impatient to leave."

The glass coffee pot sat in its heated nest on a table. Several vending machines stood adjacent to it, offering snacks of candy and cold sandwiches.

"You are going to visit family, aren't you?" The woman filled Leah's cup, then turned to the two she had brought.

"Yes, my brother Lonnie." The heat from the hot liquid flowed through the sides of the cup. Leah held it gingerly. Her hazel eyes turned to the windows and the slowly sinking sun. Impatiently she flicked her light brown hair behind her shoulder.

"Perhaps you should telephone him and explain about the delay," the woman suggested.

"There's no need." Leah gave a brief shake of her head. "He doesn't know I'm coming. It's a surprise for his birthday tomorrow." She glanced at the persistently moving hands of the clock. "At least, I hope it will be. First I have to get there."

"What's your brother doing in Austin? I mean," the woman laughed, "there are quite a few other towns in Nevada I would pick first."

"His letter indicated that it wasn't a bustling metropolis," Leah smiled. "He's only there temporarily, though. He works for a mining company. He's part of a team and they sent him to Austin to do some tests in the area."

The coffee pot was set back in place. "What about the rest of your family?" The woman picked up the cups and began wandering toward the reception counter, her gaze resting curiously on the attractive young woman walking beside her.

"There's only my parents. They're in Alaska now." At the woman's lifted brow, Leah explained, "Dad is in the Air Force."

"That explains why someone as young as you is so accustomed to flying," the woman replied.

Twenty-two didn't feel so young, but it probably seemed young to the brunette, who was in her late thirties. Nor did Leah correct the woman's suggestion that she was flying from habit. Time was the key factor in her choice of transportation and it was slipping away.

"How much longer do you think it will be before we leave?" Leah glanced at the clock, her impatience returning.

The woman shrugged, setting down one of the cups

to open the counter door. "I don't know. As soon as Mr. Smith arrives, I suppose."

The answer was hardly welcome. She had been waiting for the last two hours. His tardiness seemed to be upsetting only herself. Everyone else seemed to accept it as natural, but then he was a frequent customer of this charter flying service.

Settling on to the vinyl-covered couch, Leah acknowledged that the worst thing that could happen would be for Mr. Smith not show up. Her portion of the chartered flight to Austin had virtually emptied her meager savings account. Only by sharing the cost of plane and pilot with this Mr. Smith had she been able to afford the flight.

Luck had been sitting on her shoulder the day she had called to inquire about the price. When she had been told how much it would be, Leah had been ready to shelve the idea as too expensive. Then an inquiry as to when she wanted to go prompted the discovery that a charter flight had already been booked for that Friday with the same destination.

Leah had been on pins and needles until it was confirmed that Mr. Smith was willing to share the expense. With a sigh she admitted that the waiting wasn't over yet.

A connecting door into the waiting lounge opened and a man stuck his head inside the room. Brown hair had begun to recede from his wide forehead, creased now with a studious frown of absent concentration.

"Hey, Mary, have you heard any more from Reilly since he called to say he'd be late?"

"Sorry, Grady." The brunette lifted her hands in an open-palmed gesture. "Haven't heard a word."

He signed. "What about my other passenger?"

"She's here." The receptionist motioned toward Leah sitting on the couch.

His gaze swung the width of the room to Leah. Immediately that distant look left his expression. He stepped into the room, a smile splitting his broad cheeks.

"You are Miss Talbot?" His smile deepened at Leah's answering nod. "Well, this is a pleasant surprise. I was afraid I was going to be stuck with a toddering old maid who would be scared to death of flying." He thrust a large hand out to her. "I'm Grady Thompson, your pilot."

"How do you do, Mr. Thompson," Leah replied as her hand was wrung in a vigorous shake.

"No, make it Grady," the pilot insisted with a bright twinkle in his eyes.

He was of medium height with a stocky frame. The paunch around his waist became more noticable as he sat on the couch beside her. He was in his forties, old enough to be her father, but that didn't stop him from flirting. Yet his rakish, good-natured charm made it impossible for Leah to feel offended or repulsed.

"Okay, Grady," she smiled naturally. Her light brown hair caught the golden fire of the sunlight streaming through the windows.

He studied the streaks of gold for a second, then shifted his gaze to her classic profile, partially outlined as she turned to him. None of her features was striking, not the arching curve of brow, nor the bright gleam in her hazel eyes or the healthy glow of her complexion. Yet the total picture was decidedly attractive.

"If you're calling me Grady," the pilot tipped his head to the side, "I can't keep calling you Miss Talbot."

"It's Leah," answering the question he had only implied.

"Tell me, Leah, are you a friend of Reilly's?"

"Reilly is Mr. Smith?" A brow arched briefly to confirm her guess.

"Obviously you don't know him," Grady chuckled. "If you aren't a friend of Reilly's then what's taking you out to the middle of Nevada's nowhere?"

"I'm going to see my brother—providing your Mr. Smith shows up," Leah added wryly.

"Reilly is not anybody's Mr. Smith."

The dry undertone of his voice aroused Leah's curiosity. "It sounds as though you know him quite well." Tactfully she pried for more information about her mysterious, and late, flying companion.

The pilot took a long, considering breath and leaned against the back cushion of the couch. "I think the whole point is just the opposite. I doubt if anyone knows Reilly 'quite well.' He's a law unto himself, a lone wolf. He's part Indian, which may account for it."

"Oh, I see," Leah murmured. "Why is he going to Austin?"

"Business. He has connections with some of the

mining interests around Austin and Tonopah. I usually fly him to one place or the other," was the reply.

Fleetingly Leah wondered if this Reilly Smith worked for the same company that her brother Lonnie did. It was also entirely possible that he worked for one of their competitors. No matter, Leah shrugged inwardly. The only thing she was really interested in was when was Mr. Reilly Smith going to show up.

"Do you live here in Las Vegas?" Grady changed the subject to one that interested him more.

"Yes." Before the usual question could be asked, Leah added, "I'm a secretary to one of the executives of a local bank," and hoped Grady wouldn't add the usual comment that she would look good in one of the chorus lines that were the trademark of the lavish shows at the hotels on the strip.

"And your brother lives in Austin?"

"Only for the time being." Leah went on to explain his temporary assignment in Austin.

"Has it been a while since you've seen him?"

"No, we were together at Christmas, but tomorrow is his birthday and I wanted to surprise him."

"You must think a lot of him to go to all this expense," Grady observed.

"Lonnie and I are very close," agreed Leah.

Left unspoken were the details of her hopscotch childhood, skipping from one end of the world to the other. Under those circumstances, it was natural that she and Lonnie would be close. Despite the years that separated their ages, they were like twins.

"What's your boyfriend have to say about all this? And don't tell me a girl like you doesn't have at least one boyfriend," the pilot teased with a knowing wink.

'Let's just say that he questioned my sanity." A self-mocking laugh accompanied her reply as Leah remembered Marv's reaction.

He too worked in the accounting department of the same bank as she did. She hadn't decided yet where their relationship was going, so for want of a better word, she accepted the classification of Marv as her boyfriend.

In truth, none of her co-workers nor her roommate Nancy had actually encouraged the trip. They had all claimed that they understood her desire to see her brother again, but none of them seemed to think it was wise to spend all of her savings for that goal.

Of course, they didn't seem to possess that close feeling of kinship with their brothers or sisters. If she had been spending the money to see a boyfriend, they probably wouldn't have questioned her decision. But a brother! the thought brought a wry smile to her mouth.

'Your boyfriend was probably jealous that you weren't spending the weekend with him. I would be." Again Grady ran an admiring eye over her features.

Leah darted a quick glance at the wall clock. "I'm beginning to think I won't be going anywhere this weekend," she sighed.

Reaching into her bag, she removed the opened pack of cigarettes and tapped out a filter-tip. As she started to search for the lighter, a flame sprang from the match in Grady's hand. She smiled her thanks and placed the cigarette between her peach-tinted lips, bending her head toward the flame.

"Don't worry, Reilly will be here. If there was a question that he might not make it, he would have said so when he called earlier," the pilot assured her. "In the meantime, why don't I take your luggage out to the plane and stow it in the baggage compartment?"

"Okay," Leah agreed. "At least, I'll be one step closer to leaving."

With a cheering smile, Grady patted her knee. "Don't give up. We'll make it off the ground yet."

Then he was picking up her blue weekender bag and the cosmetic case and walking toward the door leading to the hangar apron. With his departure, the minutes started to drag again.

The smoke from her cigarette spiralled above her head. Inhaling briefly on the filter-tip, Leah exhaled more smoke impatiently. The blue-gray cloud swirled upward.

The outside door opened. Her gaze swung indifferently toward the sound, expecting to see the pilot returning. It was a stranger who entered.

Her mind had a preconceived idea of what Reilly Smith would look like—in his late forties, a supposition based on the belief that only an older, senior member of a mining team would charter an aircraft, short and stocky in build.

This man didn't meet the description. He was six

foot, leanly built but not slender and roughly ten years younger, in his mid-thirties. Jet black hair framed the boldly defined features of his bronzed tan face, prominent cheekbones leanly hollowing to powerful jawline. A face carved by the wind and sun.

His dress was a casual leisure suit of rugged brown denim. A complementing shirt patterned in yellow and brown was open at the throat revealing the large nugget of turquoise attached to the beaten silver choker around his neck.

Despite this contrast between the man and her image, Leah was certain this was Reilly Smith. The quiet pride of his carriage, the sensation of aloofness, and the effortless, animal stride convinced her she was right.

Mary, the dark-haired receptionist, confirmed it. "Finally you arrive, Mr. Smith!" Her hands rested akimbo on her hips. "Miss Talbot was about to decide you were a figment of her imagination."

For the first time since entering the waiting lounge, his gaze acknowledged her presence in the room. His eyes were startlingly green, the smooth, impenetrable color of jade.

A disturbing shiver of awareness trembled through Leah as his cool gaze appraised her assets, admired them openly, then smoothly dismissed them in favor of the business at hand.

"I was delayed," he said, which was neither an explanation nor an apology. "My cases are sitting outside. Are you ready to leave, Miss Talbot?"

After waiting for going on three hours, Leah

marvelled that he had the nerve to ask if *she* was ready! Sharply snubbing out her cigarette in the ashtray, she suppressed the impulse to remind him that he was the one who was late.

She kept her reply to a calm, "My luggage is already in the plane, Mr. Smith." But the clasp of her handbag snapped shut rather loudly as she closed it and rose to her feet.

Stepping outside the building, a desert wind tugged at the hem of her camel-colored skirt, briefly lifting it to reveal a shapely leg. Leah held the open front of her matching tunic-styled waistcoat together with one hand while her other hand carrying the bag tried to keep the teasing wind from billowing her skirt.

As an afterthought, she realized that she probably should have worn slacks. Habits die hard, and she had lived in too many foreign countries where slacks on women were viewed with disfavor.

Her shoes clicked loudly on the concrete while the man walking beside her made barely any sound at all. A sideways glance noticed that her heels didn't gain her much height. The top of her head came somewhere around his chin.

Automatically her gaze slid to the left hand carrying his bags. There was no wedding band on his finger. Somehow Leah had known there wouldn't be—perhaps because of Grady's statement that Reilly Smith was a lone wolf.

Shifting her gaze straight ahead, Leah mused silently that there were probably a lot of girls who would like to change his status. He was a compellingly handsome man. Not that it mattered to her. She was making this trip to see her brother.

A few yards ahead, Grady was standing beside the orange and white wing of a Cessna 310. The twin engine plane looked sleek and racy. A smile flashed across the pilot's face as he saw their approach.

"Didn't I tell you he'd make it, Leah?" he declared in a hearty voice, then to the man at her side, "Hello, Reilly."

"Hello, Grady." It was a warm and friendly voice, unlike the impersonal tone Leah had heard earlier. A brisk handshake followed the exchange of greetings.

"Let me stow your gear." Grady reached for the two bags gripped in the man's left hand.

"I'll take the briefcase on board." Reilly Smith relinquished only the larger of the two bags, retaining the attaché case. His green eyes made an arc in the deepening lavender sky. A single star winked feebly in the purple twilight. "What's it look like up ahead, Grady?"

The pilot briefly scanned the sky, then shrugged and returned his attention to his passengers. "There's a front moving in. We still have a chance of reaching Austin before it does. If not, it might get a little rough, but we'll make it." With his free hand, Grady motioned toward the open door of the plane. "Climb aboard."

The two small steps made it easy for Leah to climb on the wing even in her skirt. Maneuvering past the front seat to the second seats was more awkward. Reilly Smith followed with an ease that she envied.

He sat down in the seat beside her. Considering the apparent friendliness between himself and the pilot, Leah had partially expected him to sit in front with Grady. As she fastened her seat belt, she noticed the brief case he had brought on board and realized he probably intended to work.

Grady climbed agilely aboard and swung himself into the pilot's seat directly ahead of Leah. His quick glance encompassed both of them before he buckled his seat belt.

"Did you two introduce yourselves?" The question didn't break the rhythm of his pre-flight checklist.

"More or less," Leah answered.

"She's flying to Austin to visit her brother." The information was given as the first of the plane's engines growled to life, the propeller hesitating, then spinning into a blur.

Leah cast a sideways glance at her companion. "My brother works for a mining company. He's part of a team that's been temporarily assigned to survey the Austin area." This seemed like an excellent opportunity to see if Reilly Smith was a member of the same company or with a rival firm. "Grady mentioned that you had connections with some mining interests. Perhaps you know my brother. His name is Lonnie Talbot."

There was a disconcerting levelness to his jade eyes as they briefly met her look. The grooves at each side of his hard mouth deepened into a faint smile.

"No, I don't know him."

The roar of both engines made conversation

impossible. Leah was forced to set aside her curiosity for the time being. At least she felt secure in the assumption that Reilly Smith did not work for the same company as her brother.

In the pilot's seat, Grady was on the radio. "McCarren Ground Control, this is 92 George requesting taxi instructions."

Excitement danced in her veins. After all the waiting, she was finally on her way. Looking out the window, Leah smiled with secret amusement at what Lonnie's reaction would be when he learned she had flown to be with him on his birthday.

Blue lights flashed outside her window as the plane rolled along the taxi strip to the airport runway. At the edge of the runway, the engines roared with thundering force as Grady made his run-up. Then the tower radioed permission for them to take off.

Grady half-looked over his shoulder, a grin on his otherwise serious face. "Now we'll get this bird off the ground."

Smoothly the plane pivoted on to the runway, the engines building power. Leah felt the surge of acceleration as the brakes were released and the throttle opened to full power. The nose was lifted off the ground. Seconds later the plane was airborne and climbing, the landing gear thumping into the belly.

Outside her window, Leah could see the blaze of city lights in the pre-night darkness. The brilliant neon lights of the hotels and casinos on Las Vegas's famous strip were like an iridescently colored ribbon.

Cool night air from the vent above her head ruffled

the light brown wings of her hair. The infra-red lights on the instrument panel kept the darkness at bay, those lights and the reading light shining down on the seat next to hers.

Her fellow passenger was not gazing at the diminishing world below them, Leah noticed. His briefcase was opened on his lap. Common courtesy ruled that she shouldn't try to resume their conversation when he was obviously working. The urge was strong to look over his shoulder and see the contents of the papers he was studying. She resisted, averting her attention again to the window. Eventually the only thing she could see was her own reflection.

She considered taking out the paperback book she had brought in her bag, then decided against it. She was too intent on reaching her destination to concentrate on reading.

The airplane levelled off. Grady partially turned in his seat. "Want to sit up front with me for a while, Leah?"

"Thank you, yes," she agreed readily. Conversation would make the time pass faster.

As Leah unbuckled her seat belt, Grady smiled crookedly at the man sitting next to her. "You don't have any objections to the switch, do you, Reilly?"

"None at all." There was a faint mockery in the reply as silently laughing green eyes flicked a glance at Leah.

Briefly she wondered if Reilly Smith thought she was making a play for the pilot. Surely he could see that Grady was old enough to be her father.

"Don't bump into any of the controls," Grady cautioned as Leah crouched in a half-erect position to negotiate the tiny aisle way to the empty front seat.

A helping hand gripped her elbow. With faint surprise, she realized it belonged to Reilly Smith. His touch was pleasantly strong and reassuring, but brief.

Dodging the control panel near the floor, Leah slid on to the right front seat, straightening her skirt over her knees. The change of seats had been accomplished without mishap despite the close quarters.

"Thank you," she offered over her shoulder for the steadying hand. "I hope Grady and I talking won't disturb your work, Mr. Smith."

"As a matter of fact, I think I'll quit for a while and get some sleep." The snap of the briefcase lid followed his statement.

When the reading light went off, Leah fleetingly wished she had not moved from her seat. She would have liked to satisfy some of her curiosity about this Reilly Smith.

"It's amazing." Grady shook his head, a wry smile on his face.

"What is?" Leah returned blankly.

"Him." With a backward nod of his head, the pilot indicated the man in the seat behind Leah.

Self-consciously she was aware that Grady's voice carried easily to the man. She glanced over her shoulder to see Reilly Smith's reaction to the comment. He was leaning back in his seat, eyes closed. His chest moved in an even rhythm.

'He's already asleep.' Grady sighed. "He just closes his eyes. No tossing, no turning, just sleep.'

'Must be nice,'' Leah agreed, settling back into her seat. She glanced around at the instrument dials illuminated by the infra-red light. "Is the plane on auto-pilot now?''

'Yup.'' But Leah noticed the automatic way Grady kept checking the panel. "Have you ever been in the front seat of a private plane before?''

'My dad has taken me up several times, but never in anything as sophisticated as this,'' she admitted.

'Modern avionics courtesy of the computer age.' Grady smiled. "It does everything but land the plane. and nearly does that. It's great, but all equipment breaks down eventually. Let's not talk about flying, though—I hear that all day long. Considering your young years and the length of this flight, I think there's time for you to tell me about your childhood.'

'It won't take long,' Leah laughed softly. "My brother and I were Air Force brats.'' She added a sketchy outline of her childhood life, moving from air base to air base.

'How in heaven's name did you wind up in Las Vegas?''

'The usual way. Dad was transferred to Nellis Air Force Base when I was in high school. I had graduated and just started a secretarial course when his orders came through for Alaska. I wanted to finish my training, so for that reason, and because it was time to leave the nest, I stayed.'

"The lure of the bright lights?'' Grady mocked.

"Not a bit. I'm very happy being a secretary," she stated positively. "I have no desire to be an entertainer of any sort. The work is too hard and the hours are too demanding."

"That's true enough," he agreed. "Are you like the rest of the Las Vegas residents, rarely stepping inside a gambling casino unless you work there?"

"Exactly!" Then she qualified her answer. "When new shows open or a favorite celebrity of mine is appearing, I do go then. But on the whole, I leave the casinos for the tourists and the gamblers."

"Say," Grady paused, turning a curious look to her, "did you tell me that you were in the South Pacific for a time?"

"Guam and Hawaii."

"I was there when I was in the service—and I'm not going to tell you how long ago that was!"

A steady flow of questions began as Grady probed her memory to see if she had been to places he had visited, then compared her descriptions to what he remembered.

Gradually they talked themselves out and drifted into silence. Leah gazed beyond her window reflection at the star-sprinkled sky in the east. She felt sublimely relaxed.

"If you feel like nodding off," Grady spoke quietly, "you can crawl back to your old seat. At least there, you can stretch your legs out without fear of bumping any controls."

With a contented sigh, she agreed. "I think I'll do that."

It was a bit easier negotiating the tiny aisle, although Leah took care not to waken the sleeping Reilly. As she turned to slide into her seat, she noticed the inky blankness of the sky directly ahead.

"It's very dark ahead, isn't it?" she questioned Grady softly.

"It must be frontal system. I think I'll check with the weather bureau and see if I can get an update on it."

He made the call while she buckled her seat belt. The answering transmission didn't carry clearly to her, but Grady passed the message back.

"The front beat us to Austin. You'd better buckle in tight—it might get a little rough." Then he glanced over his shoulder at the sleeping figure. "Reilly!"

"I heard you," came the quiet reply. With calm deliberation, Reilly straightened and tightened his seat belt.

"I thought you were asleep." Leah spoke without thinking.

"I was."

There was not a trace of sleepiness in his voice. She decided that he wakened as quickly as he went to sleep.

CHAPTER TWO

A black void yawned ominously around the twin engine plane. Jagged splinters of lightning rained fire in the sky. Turbulent cross-currents of air alternately tugged and pushed at the plane.

At each bone-shaking bounce of the plane, Grady throttled back to avoid putting any more stress on the structure than necessary. The buffeting only increased in intensity.

"Reilly!" Grady called for him to lean forward, not taking his eyes off the gauges and dials bouncing with the plane in front of him. The dark-haired passenger loosened his seat belt slightly and bent toward the pilot. "It's only going to get worse. I'm going to try to fly around it. Okay?" he shouted.

"Okay." The voice that agreed didn't sound at all troubled by the weather.

Leah, despite all her trust in the competency of their pilot and the airworthiness of the craft, found tremors of fear shuddering through her. She tried to forestall the guilt feeling of cowardice with knowledge that only a fool wouldn't be afraid.

Still, she held her breath as Grady slowly banked the plane toward the east, trying to outrace the storm and sneak in around it. Sliding a rounded look to the man next to her, she decided that behind that expressionless face, he must have nerves of steel.

A severe downdraught sucked at the plane, nearly taking Leah's stomach when the plane groaned free. The pitch blackness that surrounded them was only broken by fiery tongues of lightning licking the air around them. The plane continued bucking through the turbulence.

"I can't get above this stuff!" Grady shouted. "I'm going to take her down a couple of thousand feet and see if it's any calmer."

No reply was necessary. Leah doubted if her dry mouth and throat could have made any. It felt as if they were diving, but she knew it was a controlled sideslip downward.

Through the mirrorlike reflection of the window, Leah watched the pilot gently levelling the wings out. Lightning flashed ahead of them, its brilliant yellow-white light lasting for several seconds.

"Sweet Jesus!" Grady's mutter of angry prayer reached Leah's ears at the same instant that she saw the mound of solid black rising in front of the nose.

It was a mountain. She registered the terrifying fact

a second before she was thrown violently to one side as Grady executed a sharp right turn.

Another flash of lightening clearly outlined more mountains in their path.

"There aren't supposed to be any damned mountains at this altitude," came Grady's savage mutter as again he banked sharply. "This damned altimeter must—"

He didn't finish the rest. A jagged fork of lightning had briefly shown an escape route—a low saddleback ridge connecting two peaks. Grady aimed the nose of the plane at where he thought it had been. Leah waited in frozen stillness for the next streak of lightning that would reveal if his aim was true.

It was late. They were nearly there when flashing light revealed that he had misjudged the spot. The plane was going to crash into the side of the mountain.

Quickly Grady tried to correct for his error. Leah gasped silently in horror—oh, Lonnie! Fingers closed vicelike on the back of her neck, pushing her head to her knees and holding it there.

"Stay down." Reilly's softly spoken order pierced her terror.

There was a sickening jolt on the right side of the plane. The right wing tip had clipped the mountainside wrenching and tearing as half of it split away.

The plane pitched downward. "Come on, baby!" Grady urged below his breath.

The belly of the plane bounced and thudded on solid ground. It sliced along for a few rattling feet, then the right wing again met an immovable object.

Their speed sent the plane spinning like a top across the ground.

The screaming rip of metal seemed to surround Leah on all sides without end. Why was it all happening so slowly, her mind cried! Glass shattered above her head. There were more tearing, crunching sounds of metal from her side—the left side.

There was a faint sensation of pain as blackness swirled in front of her eyes. Yet Leah remained semiconscious, dissociated from what was happening. The roaring in her ears deafened her to all outside sounds.

Then the black mist began to recede. An iron hook of some kind was pulling her upward. A second later she realized it wasn't an iron hook, but a muscled arm.

"Come on. We've got to get out of here." The firm voice seemed to come from some great distance.

But Leah knew she had to obey the command. She shook her head to chase away the lingering daze. The trembling awkwardness of her legs made the arm around her ribs provide most of her support.

Taking a shaky breath, she suddenly realized she was alive. It was Reilly Smith's arm that was helping her through the open door of the downed plane. As she squeezed through the narrow opening, stumbling over the seats, she wondered why he hadn't opened the door wider.

When her foot touched the loose gravel outside the door, she knew. The plane had stopped lengthwise against the side of the mountain. It was the mountain.

wall that wouldn't allow the door to open more than it was.

Wind whipped at her hair as she emerged. There was the sting of rain against her cheeks while thunder rumbled ominously overhead. She wanted to lean against the body of the plane and quietly sob her relief and gratitude at being alive, but the arm around her waist wouldn't let her.

"We can't stop here," Reilly denied.

Accepting that there was wisdom in what he said, Leah didn't protest his guidance. The numbness was leaving her legs. Walking was still difficult over the uneven ground because of the high heels of her shoes.

Some distance from the plane, he halted in an open patch of mountain desert. The supporting arm was removed to press a hand on her shoulder, pushing her to the ground.

"You wait here," he ordered. "I'm going back to the plane. And stay down, or you'll make a good target for the lightning."

Leah nodded, then found her voice. "I will." As he pivoted to leave her, she remembered. "Where's Grady?"

There was no answer as her rescuer glided away into the dark. Perhaps he hadn't heard the question, she decided, or else he was going back to get the pilot.

Lightning crackled. In the illuminating light, she could see his shadowy outline. Beyond was the mutilated metal body of the plane. She shuddered at the miracle that they had survived in that wreckage.

The tiny pellets of wind-whipped rain could hardly

be called a downpour, but as Leah waited in the darkness, she could feel the rain slowly soaking her clothes. She pulled the camel-colored waistcoat closer together.

A shooting pain stabbed her left arm. Experimentally her right hand explored the area of pain. The sleeve of her blouse was wetly sticky and warm. Then her fingers felt the tear in the material and the gash in the soft flesh of her upper arm. She didn't remember being hurt. Instinctively her hand clutched the wound, checking the flow of blood. In this darkness she couldn't see how serious it might be. Only now that she had discovered it was it beginning to throb. Suddenly Leah felt very cold and very alone.

Her gaze tried to penetrate the black curtain of night for a glimpse of the man who had led her here. There was only the ghostly shimmer of white from the painted metal of the aircraft.

Thunder boomed. A flash of lightning followed before the rolling thunder stopped. Leah had promised to wait, but if Reilly Smith didn't return soon, she wasn't going to keep that promise.

An eerie pool of light was coming from the direction of the plane, floating along the ground through the desert scrub. It was several spine-chilling seconds before Leah realized it was coming from a flashlight. A sighing laugh slipped from her throat.

She could distinguish enough of the tall figure to see that he was carrying something over his shoulder. Grady? She waited, breathlessly, for the man to reach her.

Blinded by the light when it picked her out in the darkness, she shielded her eyes from the glare. The light moved away as the figure knelt beside her, swinging the burden from his shoulder. Leah stared at the bundle—a coat with its sleeves tied together to carry the loose objects inside.

"Where's Grady?" Her hazel eyes bored into the expressionless male face as she mentally braced herself for his answer.

"He's dead." Long fingers deftly untying the coat sleeves.

"No!" she whispered even as she accepted the truth of his statement. It wasn't something to lie about. She tried to swallow back the tremor in her voice. "You didn't leave him in the plane?"

"Yes." The rain bronzed his tanned features into a mask. The green eyes held no hint of grief in their jade depths when they swung toward her. "Let me see what I can do for your arm."

Absently Leah touched her wound, its throbbing vaguely uncomfortable. It seemed wrong to have left Grady in that gnarled mess of twisted metal. It was harder to adjust to the fact that he was dead, that warm, vital man.

"You'll have to hold the flashlight." When his words brought no response from Leah, Reilly frowned. Sooty lashes thickened by the rain narrowed his gaze. "Snap out of it!"

"W-What?" she blinked.

"I said you'll have to hold the flashlight so I can look at your arm," he repeated curtly.

Her hazel eyes had started to mist with tears. She hurriedly blinked them away as her fingers closed over the cold wet metal of the flashlight. She directed the beam at her injury. Beyond the radiating circle, she saw Reilly Smith remove his pocket knife and open the blades.

"I'm going to rip the sleeve the rest of the way." With the explanation given, the blade sliced through the material's seam. A quick rip and the sleeve was in his hand.

Using the remnants, he carefully wiped away the blood to see the extent of the cut. The jagged rip in her flesh wasn't a pleasant sight and Leah turned her gaze away. She could feel him probing the wound for any splinters of glass or metal. It throbbed with burning fire now.

He turned away, opening the metal lid of a large first aid kit he had placed at his side. He took out a bottle of antiseptic and closed the lid before the rain could damage any of the contents. Water droplets glistened like diamonds in his jet black hair.

"This is going to hurt," he warned.

Although prepared, Leah couldn't stop herself from emitting a choked gasp of pain as her arm jerked to avoid the fiery liquid.

"Hold still!"

"It hurts!" she snapped back, stating the obvious.

Reilly Smith ignored that. "And hold the light still so I can see what I'm doing."

Insensitive pig! Leah thought angrily. At least he

could have said he was sorry but that he couldn't help hurting her.

Gritting her teeth, she focused the light again on her arm. This time she didn't cry out as he poured the antiseptic on the open wound, although the flashlight beam did waver slightly. Next came the bandage, which was expertly and efficiently accomplished.

"Thank you," Leah offered as some of the pain began to recede.

"You're welcome." A distant smile touched his mouth.

He took the flashlight and laid it on the ground, bathing their clearing with light. Unfolding the coat on the ground, he slipped a pistol into the waistband of his brown slacks and pulled his jacket over it to keep out the rain. A canteen and another small box were set aside along with a folded square of red material. He stood up, shaking out the coat.

"This will keep the rain off of you," he said, holding it out to Leah.

"In case you haven't noticed, I'm already soaked." She hugged her arms tighter around her waist, feeling the biting chill of her damp clothes.

"I don't want the bandage getting wet." He draped a man's raincoat over her shoulders, drawing the collar around her neck. "At night, it's cold in the mountain desert—in the spring or any other time of year. It will give you some protection against the cold if not the rain."

What she wanted was some dry clothes, but logically Leah realized that they would soon get wet, too. Gingerly she slid her injured arm in a sleeve and carefully eased her other arm into the second sleeve and buttoned the coat.

'Whose is this?'' she asked unthinkingly as the coat drowned her in its looseness.

"Grady's."

Leah paled. Suddenly the coat didn't feel the same. She started to unbutton it.

'You can wear it,'' she murmured tightly.

'No.'' His voice was firm as his watchful eyes studied her face. "He isn't going to object, Miss Talbot.''

Her temper flared at his apparently flippant remark. "How can you be so callous?''

"It's the truth—however hard it may sound,'' Reilly Smith replied calmly. Her anger flowed over him without denting his aloof composure. "There isn't anything more we can do for Grady. Our main concern now has to be ourselves. We'll have to use what's on hand to survive the night.''

His cold logic defeated her anger. She began rebuttoning the coat. "You could build a fire to warm us up and dry us out,'' she declared, a seed of rebellion remaining.

"It's raining,'' he reminded her dryly.

'Well,'' impatiently she pushed the wet brown hair away from her forehead, ''you are part Indian. Surely it shouldn't be too difficult for you.''

An eyebrow lifted in a measuring look. Her teeth nibbled self-consciously on her lower lip. That had sounded very prejudiced and she hadn't meant it at all that way. His composure had got under her skin and made her thoughtless in her reply.

He reached down and picked up the folded red square. "A fire could be built," there was a hint of cynical amusement in his voice, "after I'd found some dry wood and started the kindling in the rain. Maybe after a couple of hours, I would have a fire blazing—if the two of us hadn't succumbed to exposure and shock, we might enjoy it."

"I'm sorry, I didn't think." Leah lowered her gaze to the ground. She took a deep breath and let it out slowly. "We can't sit out here in the rain. Wouldn't we be better off in the plane?"

"The metal of the plane would act like a lightning rod. It's too dangerous." The square of red was shaken out, rustling stiffly in protest. The opposite side of the material resembled aluminium. Its silvery finish glistened in the flashlight beam. "Besides, higher up the mountain there are some loose tailings from an abondoned mine. The rain might bring it down and block the door by morning. Out here, we might get wet and cold—it wouldn't be any warmer in the plane—but we wouldn't be trapped inside the mangled wreckage."

Again, Leah had to submit to the wisdom of his reasoning. But she was wet and cold, and getting colder. Her teeth had started to chatter and her arm was beginning to stiffen and feel sore.

"What are we going to do?" Her gaze wearily moved to him . Since all her thoughts seemed to have been wrong, it was time he suggested something.

"Stand up."

His hand was at her elbow, lifting her upright. Leah stood, waiting uncertainly for his next move. The thin, blanket-size sheet was partially wrapped around her, rising above her head in a stiff half-hood.

"Hold the side," Reilly instructed, pushing an edge of the material into her fingers. He hesitated, drawing her curious gaze. "What we're going to do is wrap ourselves together in this blanket, using our body heat to keep us warm and the blanket to keep out as much of the rain as possible."

"You're saying we should sleep together." Leah repeated the essence of his words. She was shivering and trying to keep her teeth from chattering too loudly. "It's the logical and practical thing to do, isn't it?" she added wryly.

"Yes," he nodded with a faint smile on his wet face.

She was too cold and wet and miserable to care that her straitlaced parents would be horrified to learn their daughter was sleeping under the same blanket with a virtual stranger.

"By all means, let's do it." she agreed, weakly returning his smile.

An arm slid around the bulky folds of the raincoat at her waist as he drew the stiff blanket behind and around him. At his signal, they eased themselves to the ground in unison.

Reilly lay on his back, drawing Leah's head and shoulders on his chest and curving the rest of her against his length. Pellets of rain struck at the blanket, hammering to get in, but the waterproof material kept them dry.

At first she was conscious only of the cold wetness of his hard form, then gradually she felt his body warmth steaming through his soaked clothes and she snuggled closer, shivering uncontrollably. His hands began rubbing her back, shoulders and waist, stimulating her circulation while taking care to avoid her injured arm that throbbed dully now.

"Is that better?" Warm breath stirred the air near her forehead.

"Much better." She inhaled deeply in contentment. The musky scent of his maleness was heightened by the rain.

His hands maintained their slow, steady rhythm. A small fire was glowing inside her. She was beginning to feel human again. Her mind stopped dwelling on her physical discomfort and started to wander on to other subjects.

"A search party will start looking for us tomorrow, won't they?" she said quietly.

"Yes."

"How long do you think it will take them to find us?"

"It's hard to say," For a minute Leah thought that was the only reply Reilly was going to make, then he enlarged upon his answer. "There wasn't time for a mayday call to give our location. Grady had his hands full trying to keep from nosing into the side of the mountain. If he filed a flight plan, he flew off-course trying to avoid the center of the storm. A search would initially cover the planned route, then widen its area if the plane wasn't found.''

''Then it could be late tomorrow before they find us?''

A moment of slight hesitation followed her question. ''There's a lot of rugged terrain a party would have to cover. It could be Sunday—or Monday.''

Leah shuddered, this time not from the cold. ''I'm glad I didn't let Lonnie know I was coming. He won't be worrying about me for a while anyway, wondering if I'm dead or alive.''

The authorities would first notify her parents. They, in turn, would contact her brother. With luck, by then she would be rescued.

'You were planning to surprise him?''

Leah nodded, her cheek moving against the damp denim of his jacket. ''For his birthday. It's tomorrow,'' she sighed, then pulled her mind away from its depressing path. ''You were expected, weren't you?''

''Yes, by some business friends.''

'Who do you work for?'' She tipped her head back against his shoulder, peering through the darkness of their cocoon for a glimpse of his face. The suggestion of intimacy at being in his arms seemed to banish the need for diplomatically worded questions. Her curiosity surfaced without disguise. ''An arch rival of the mining firm that employs my brother?''

''I work for myself,'' he replied.

''You own a mining company?''

''No.'' There was amused patience in his low voice. ''I design jewelry.''

As Leah digested the information, she remembered the nugget of turquoise he wore around his neck. "Turquoise jewelry?"

"Or Indian jewelry, whichever you prefer to call it." The mockery was unmistakable in his tone.

Leah stiffened defensively. "I didn't mean my comment to sound derogatory earlier. I was cold and wet and thought a fire would be the logical remedy. I simply didn't know how to build one—not from scratch." She hesitated, irritated that he had even indirectly referred to her thoughtlessly cutting remark earlier. "Grady had mentioned that you were part Indian. I only referred to it because I thought you would have the experience at building fires which I didn't have."

"You didn't need to explain. I'd already guessed that," Reilly Smith returned complacently.

Sputtering inwardly, Leah longed to demand why he had let her make the apology if, as he said, he had already guessed. It was pointless to begin an argument about it, though, since initially the fault had been hers.

"Then why were you flying to Austin?" Leah swallowed her irritation and switched to a less personal topic.

"There are turquoise mines in the vicinity that I periodically visit," he said with a thread of indulgence. "I deal directly with them, purchasing the stones I want to use for mounting."

"I didn't know that." She frowned slightly, trying to remember if Lonnie had mentioned the turquoise mines in one of his letters. "About the mines being there, I mean."

"There's a line of turquoise deposits that runs almost directly down the center of the State, starting around Battle Mountain through Austin. At Tonopah it curves north-west. The line would look like a 'J' if you drew it on a map."

"I guess I always thought most of the turquoise was found in Arizona."

"Arizona does produce quite a bit, but mostly as a by-product of their copper mining." His fingers gently pulled her long, wet hair free of the coat collar, smoothing it over her back. "I think it's time we got some sleep. It's going to be long day tomorrow."

The truth was Leah didn't want to stop talking. As long as her mind was occupied with other things, it couldn't dwell on the crash.

"I suppose you're right." she sighed reluctantly, adding a silent "again" to the admission. Her eyelids were beginning to feel heavy. "What time is it?"

"Nearing midnight. I imagine. Are you comfortable?"

"Yes," she nodded, nestling her head closer to his chest. "Goodnight."

"Goodnight."

Silence closed in. Despite the crash of thunder and lightning and the tapping of rain, it was silence. There were none of the sounds of cars and people or streetlights shining through the window that usually lulled her to sleep.

The ground was hard and unyeilding beneath her

hip. Her pillow, Reilly's chest, rose and fell in even breathing. The steady rhythm of his heart beat against her ear.

If things had been different, she would have been sleeping in a strange bed tonight, but none as alien as this. And Lonnie would have been close by. Her throat tightened as she remembered that if things had been different, Grady would be alive, too.

"If we'd left earlier," she murmured in a low, choked voice, "we could have beaten the storm to Austin."

"You would be with your brother. I would be with my friends and Grady wouldn't be dead." Leah could feel the vibration of Reilly's low-pitched voice against her ear, unemotional and aloof. "That isn't the way it is. It's best that you accept that."

Tears slid down her cheeks as she bitterly admitted he was right again. But it didn't make it any easier to accept. Her lashes fluttered down, clinging to the tears on her lower lashes.

In the night, her troubled and uneasy sleep was interrupted by a rolling roar that seemed to vibrate the ground beneath them. She stirred, her eyes opening in a frowning blink.

"What was that?" she whispered bewilderedly. She tried to raise herself up on an elbow, but the arm around her tightened and a hand pressed her head against his chest.

"It's nothing to worry about," Reilly answered quietly. "Go back to sleep."

Not fully awake and with her muscles stiffly protesting any need for movement, Leah obeyed. It was probably just the thunder anyway, she told herself.

CHAPTER THREE

It wasn't thunder.

The morning sun was in her eyes, but the light didn't blind Leah to the mound of chipped rock and rubble in front of her. A landslide had completely covered the plane.

Farther up the mountain slope on a rocky ledge, her gaze noted the black hole of a mine entrance. A fallen timber lay across in the opening, supporting only its own weight. Last night's rain had sent the loose tailings from the mine down the slope.

Leah remembered Reilly's warning about it. If they had taken shelter in the plane, they would have been trapped inside or smothered by the gravel debris.

This morning her bones ached from sleeping on the hard surface of the ground and her muscles were cramped from clinging to the warmth of Reilly's body. Yet somewhere under that mound of rock was the plane, and her discomfort seemed like a very small thing.

Soberly she watched Reilly Smith carefully working his way over the rubble. At each step, the ground shifted beneath his feet, miniature slides of loose gravel rolling away. Then he stopped, kneeling gingerly to push away the rock.

A patch of white was revealed and made larger. Using the length of his left arm as a barricade, he held back the gravel that tried to recover the patch. With painstaking slowness he pushed more rock away with his free hand, digging downward along the side of the plane.

His goal was the baggage compartment in the crumpled nose of the plane. The crash had buckled the door, popping it partly open at the bottom. Leah watched Reilly straining with only one free hand to open it the rest of the way.

When the last fragment of latch released itself, he quickly lifted it up, using it instead of his arm to hold back the gravel. Reaching inside, he wasted no time in dragging out his suitcase, then Leah's two pieces of luggage.

Gravel danced around both sides of the door in warning. He shoved the cases away, letting the rolling rocks carry them away from the plane. Leah held her breath as he slowly lowered the door. The trickle of rocks grew steadily louder as the angle lessened.

Above him, there was an uneasy shifting of rocks, but no fresh slide started when the door was down and immediately covered by slow-moving gravel. Turning, he inched his way down the slope in a half-sitting position to the luggage.

When he stood on firm ground again, Leah let out the breath she had been holding in a relieved sigh. Reilly picked up all three cases and walked to where she stood a safe distance away.

"Now we can change out of these clothes." The grooves around his mouth deepened to suggest a smile.

'I can hardly wait, agreed Leah definitely. Although she had dried out considerably from her soaking last night, her clothes still felt vaguely damp against her skin.

"Have you got a pair of jeans in there?" He set her bag and cosmetic case on the ground in front of her.

"Slacks," she told him.

"You'd better put them on, and some flat shoes."

Leah glanced around. The mountain side was sparsely covered with desert scrub. There was not a rock or boulder in sight large enough to use as a dressing curtain.

"Where can I change?" she asked finally.

An amused light danced in his green eyes. "Wherever you want," he shrugged.

"I mean somewhere private," Leah retorted. "I don't intend to strip in front of an audience."

"I guess you'll have to crouch behind one of the bushes, then." His expression changed to one of complete indifference as he bent to unsnap the lid of his suitcase. "I'm more interested in changing my own damp clothes than being an audience for you."

Pressing her lips tightly together, Leah knelt in front of her suitcase. Her injured left arm was held stiffly across her waist. It hurt badly this morning. She took care not to bump it accidently as she unlatched the lid and began rummaging through the bag's content for fresh underwear, slacks, and top.

"I wasn't suggesting that you would sit and applaud while I undressed," she muttered tautly.

"Oh? What were you suggesting?" Reilly mocked cynically.

"Just a desire for some degree of privacy." Leah rolled her change of clothes into a ball and placed a pair of flat-heeled loafers on top.

"You can have all the privacy our primitive surroundings will permit." His strong, lean features were impassive.

"Thank you." She flipped the lid of her suitcase shut with a snap.

Rising awkwardly with her bundle, she marched toward a thick clump of sage, her nose tilted into the air. Damn! she cursed silently. She had done it again.

His jesting remark to dress wherever she wanted had not had the suggestive meaning she thought. She had taken offence and defended her sense of modesty without cause. The indignant outburst had been unwarranted and unjustified. The result was that she had been made to look the ignorant fool.

Why do I always put my foot in my mouth? she sighed angrily.

'Miss Talbot.'

His low voice halted her steps. She turned hesitantly toward him, suddenly wary, knowing he deserved an apology yet still too angry with herself to make one that would sound sincere.

'What?'' she asked, somewhat abruptly.

''Before you put a clean blouse on, I'd like to look at your arm.''

''All right,'' she agreed, and resumed her course to the large bush.

Not until she had shed her damp clothes and put on clean underwear and the olive green pair of slacks did she realize that he wanted to look at her wound before she changed her clothes and not before she put on a clean blouse. The ripped sleeve of her blouse would have given him free access to the bandage.

The lacy edges of her brassiere accented too much the cleavage between her breasts for her to let him see her in only that. It didn't matter that it covered more than her bikini top. She looked with disfavor on the damp, rumpled blouse she had been wearing. She couldn't stand the thought of putting it on again.

'You get yourself into some fine messes sometimes, Leah Talbot!'' she muttered to herself.

Picking up the crisp olive and yellow print blouse, she wrapped it under her arms and around her breasts, holding it securely shut with her right hand. With a wry twist of her mouth she decided that she was decently covered and stepped from behind the bush.

The morning air was cool yet, sharply scented by

last night's rain with sage. A shiver danced over her bare shoulders. Leah couldn't decide whether it was from coolness or a chill of apprehension.

Reilly was in the clearing where they had spent the night, his back turned to her. He seemed to be buttoning the clean white shirt that hung down over a pair of dark blue denims. The sunlight glistened blackly on his hair.

"Do you want to look at my arm now, Mr. Smith?" Leah asked in a faintly defensive tone.

He glanced over his shoulder, then pivoted slowly, the shirt buttoned halfway. Without finishing his task, he reached down for the first aid kit.

"Yes, I will," he answered smoothly.

Leah walked toward him, holding her head proudly to hide the nervous hammerings of her heart. His gaze moved lazily to the white bra straps over her shoulders. A dull red flush crept into her cheeks.

"I misunderstood what you meant earlier. I forgot about the sleeve," she offered in self-protection.

"I realized that." A dark glow entered his jade eyes, but she couldn't tell whether or not he was laughing at her. "I was going to explain more fully what I meant, but I thought you might launch into another attack before I finished."

"I'm sorry." Leah lowered the angle of her chin by several degrees.

But Reilly was already removing the adhesive strips to examine her wound, accepting her apology without comment. The gentle probing of his fingers made her wince.

'Hurt?'' His piercing gaze slid quickly to her face.

'Of course.'' Her teeth sank into her lower lip, nibbling at it to distract her mind from the pain in her arm.

"It looks clean. Does it feel as if there's anything in it? A piece of glass?'' he questioned.

"No. It's just sore.'' Leah shook her head.

"I'll put a clean bandage on.''

She watched as he deftly changed the bandage to a fresh one. Her gaze strayed to the tanned column of his neck and the hollow of his throat where the nugget of turquoise rested. Then it was drawn down the partially unbuttoned front of his shirt where his muscled chest gleamed bronze and smooth like a statue's. It was several seconds before she realized he was finished. Caught staring, she flushed guiltily.

"Thank you.'' Her fingers tightened on her blouse as his gaze moved over her face.

"You're welcome.'' There was a mocking inclination of his dark head. Then Reilly turned his back to her. "You can put on your blouse now.'' With definite overtones of laughter in his voice, he added, "As long as you promise not to watch me tuck my shirt into my levis.''

Laughing softly, Leah promised and turned her back to him. She carefully eased her injured arm into the sleeve of her blouse, then twisted to find the other sleeve.

As she buttoned the last button, Reilly asked, 'Finished?''

"Yes, you can turn around now.'' A wide natural

smile was curving her mouth when he turned around, the dark jade of his eyes glittering brilliantly warm.

"Do you feel better?" He reached down to pick up a denim jacket lying across his suitcases.

"Clean, dry clothes are a wonderful improvement," Leah agreed. "The only way I could feel better is if I'd already had breakfast."

"The tin box sitting over there has some crackers in it," he suggested. "That's the best I can offer in the way of food until I can collect some firewood and get a fire going. There isn't much water in the canteen, so use it carefully," he cautioned.

"I will." She knelt beside the box and unlatched the lid. There was more than crackers inside. There were several packages of dried food that had to be mixed with water and sticks of beef jerky. "I didn't know that charter flights carried food survival kits."

"They don't as a rule." Reilly answered. "Grady was just superstitious."

"Superstitious? What do you mean?" Leah frowned.

"He served overseas during the Korean war. He flew light reconnaissance aircraft. Survival kits were carried almost as standard equipment," he explained. "One day Grady forgot his and his plane was hit by gunfire. He crashed in some heavy foliage, breaking a leg. Luckily he was in friendly territory, but it was almost three days before he was found. He swore he almost starved to death. After that he never went up without the kit and he was never shot down again. When he'd served his term and was released from the service he came back to the States and got a job flying. He kept on carrying a kit like this as a good luck charm.''

The partially unwrapped cellophane of crackers was in her hand. The appetite Leah had thought she had had receded. "The kit didn't bring him very much luck this time," she murmured sadly.

Reilly didn't comment on that. "I pointed out to him once that those dehydrated foods wouldn't be much use in this desert country where the most valuable commodity is water. His reply was that he'd never have to use it anyway, but this way the food wouldn't keep spoiling all the time."

Dully Leah swung her gaze to the rocky mound of earth that covered the plane. "Can't we get him out of there?"

"No. It would take men and machinery and a way of holding back the slide." She had known what his answer would be, but she needed to hear it. "I'm going to look for some wood to build a signal fire," Reilly continued, switching the subject back to their original topic. "You stay here. You'll be all right."

"Yes." Leah was still staring at the gravelike mound that covered the plane.

"Keep an eye out for search planes. I doubt if they'll be this far east so early this morning, but keep watch."

His firm voice reminded her that their concern must be for their rescue. The pilot was beyond help. Breathing in deeply, Leah returned her attention to the small package of crackers in her hand.

"I will," she promised.

·"Shout if you need me," he added.

At Leah's nod, he smiled in reassurance and started up the mountain slope toward the abondoned mine. His lithe stride chose a new path, avoiding the unstable ground of the slide. Leah watched him until he disappeared on the rocky ledge high above.

Taking care not to tear the wrapper, she opened the cracker package. The salty square tasted dry and chalky in her mouth. She ate only one and tightly wrapped the others in the package. As she picked up the canteen, Leah remembered Reilly's statement that water was valuable.

Hesitating, she took a small swig to wash the cracker down, then re-capped it. It was ironic, she thought, how a person always felt more thirsty when they knew water was scarce. The arid landscape made the nearly full canteen seem like very little.

Setting it aside, she reached for her cosmetic case. She creamed her face with cleansing lotion before applying fresh make-up. When her long hair had been brushed free of the snarls of sleep and laid about her shoulders in a silken curtain of light brown, she felt almost whole again.

Her hazel eyes, bright again with renewed spirit, scanned the western sky. Not a single cloud broke the pale blue scene. The storm clouds of last night had completely disappeared.

A bird was soaring lazily above the desert valley floor below the mountain. In the far distance, Leah could see the wispy ribbon of a jet trail. The desert seemed to stretch for endless miles. The awesome fact registered that she couldn't see one sign of human habitation, not a building and not a road.

A tremendous sense of isolation closed over her. The incredible silence of the desert mountains was loud. What if they weren't found? Before it overwhelmed her, Leah rose to her feet. She was not going to panic, she told herself. There was a search party looking for them. She was not stranded in this forbidding wilderness for ever.

She glanced at the rocky ledge where she had last seen Reilly. She wished he would come back soon. Shout if you need me, he had said. Right now, she needed to know he was still out there. But she stifled the desire to call out to him.

Activity was the answer. Sitting doing nothing, she had let her imagination run away with her. The search party would find them. It was only a matter of time. Meantime, the best thing was to occupy herself with some small task until Reilly returned. Favoring her injured arm, Leah glanced around to find that task. Her gaze fell on the damp clothes she had laid on top of her suitcase.

They would never dry in that heap. Her blouse was on top. Leah picked it up and carried it to a bush, spreading it out for the sun to dry. Then she returned for the next piece of clothing. Deliberately taking her time, she made a project out of it, smoothing out the wrinkles and spreading all four corners of the garment over the bush. It served to prolong the task.

When her clothes were laid out to dry, she started on Reilly's. She was straightening the sleeves on his brown jacket when a loosened stone rolled down the slope behind her. Turning, she saw Reilly working his way down, his arms laden with small, broken chunks of wood. The bulk of it seemed to be pieces of timber from the mine.

'Hello!'' Her greeting echoed the happiness and relief she felt at his return. Mostly it was happiness. "I see you found some wood.

"There's more up there, so we won't have to worry about wood for the time being.'' He flashed her a quick smile, the mask of aloofness gone. "I found something else, too.''

"What?'' Leah held her breath.

She sensed that whatever he had found pleased him. It was responible for the brilliant light in his eyes that seemed to radiate a satified glow over his compelling features. Maybe he had seen a road or highway on the other side of the mountain.

'Water,'' Reilly stated, dumping the wood on to the ground near the center of the clearing. He looked back up the mountain. "There's a rocky outcropping on the east side beneath a slight overhang. It's shaped like a basin. Last night's rain filled it about half full.''

'Then it's safe to drink?'' It wasn't a sign of civilization he had found, but her cottony tongue said it was nearly as good.

'It's rain water.'' The corners of his eyes crinkled to match the smile curving the male line of his mouth.

"I feel like drinking the canteen dry to celebrate,'' she laughed.

"Be my guest." He motioned toward the canteen as he kneeled beside the pile of wood.

"Now that I know I can drink, I don't feel very thirsty," she shrugged.

Reilly picked out a thin plank of wood and used it as a scraper to clear a fire circle. "Would you gather some stones to make a fire ring? Some of those near the slide will do."

Hampered by her sore arm, it was a slow job collecting the medium sized rocks to form an outer protective ring. When Reilly had the ground cleared to his satifaction, he took out his pocket knife and began splintering wood for kindling. The tiny mound of wood chips lay in the center of the circle.

"Do you have any paper?" Reilly asked.

"Some tissue in my cosmetic case," Leah volunteered.

"That should work fine." While she went to get it, he removed a box of matches from his inside jacket pocket.

She handed him one of the white tissues and watched him stuff it beneath the wood chips. Removing one match, he struck against the side of the box. He cupped the flame protectively with his hand as he carried it to the tissue and kindling. The white tissue charred, then burst into flame. A teasing breeze swirled the tiny fire.

Reilly nursed it carefully so the fire wouldn't be blown out. "If there's one guarantee in lighting a fire, it's that no matter which way the wind is blowing when you start, it will change direction the minute the fire has started." He slid a glittering look at Leah, amusement in the crooked smile. "Invariably blowing the smoke at the person who started the fire."

'Is that a piece of Indian lore?" She laughed at the truth in his comment.

'Naturally." As the kindling started to burn, Reilly added slightly larger pieces of wood, stacking them in a pyramid around and above the small flame.

There was only a small breeze blowing, a mere breath of wind. Leah looked around the clearing at the dry-looking sagebrush that stretched over the mountainside. Here and there a pinyon tree dotted the slopes, but they were very few.

"There isn't any chance of starting a grass fire, is there?" she asked, trying not to imagine the horror of trying to escape from that.

"Very little," Reilly answered. "The fire ring will keep the flames from spreading as long as the wind isn't strong. Strangely enough, it's rare to have a fire sweep through the desert, considering how dry and flammable some of the plants are."

"Why?" Leah tipped her head curiously to one side, absently tucking the opposite side of her hair behind her ear.

"Mainly because it's so dry," was his cryptic reply. Then he explained, "There's so little moisture in the desert that the plants can't grow close together. Their roots systems are wide and deep to absorb every available trace of water, so they choke out any new plant that tries to grow. The distance between plants keeps any fire that starts from spreading."

He sat back on his heels, waiting for the pyra-midlike stack of wood to catch fire. Leah understood what he had meant last night about it being a slow process to build a fire, without the aid of kerosene or starter fuel.

"Now that we've found water, we can mix up some of that dehydrated food," he stated.

"I'll see what we have." Leah opened the metal box and began looking at the packages inside. "Here's some beef stew, but what shall we heat it in?"

"There's some twisted fragments of metal from the plane wing over by the slide. Maybe one of them can be used as a makeshift pan."

"I'll see." She started to get to her feet, but he motioned her to sit back down.

"On second thoughts, I'd better look," he said. "I don't want you accidently cutting yourself on the metal edges."

He stacked two more pieces of wood, larger than those propped against each other, making sure there remained openings at the bottom to keep a circling draught of air.

Leah didn't object as he rose smoothly to his feet. With only one hand operating effectively, she had already discovered gathering rocks for the fire ring that she was very clumsy.

Within a few minutes Reilly had returned with a twisted piece of metal. Using two of the rocks around the fire, one as a hammer and one as a hard surface, he beat away the sharp edges around the outside. Then he turned the angulary hollowed center upside down on top of the rock and hammered a flat bottom in the pan. When the sides were fairly straight, he examined it for a moment, then glanced at Leah.

"Do you think it will work, cook?" A mocking eyebrow was lifted in question.

"So I'm the cook, am I?" Leah nodded in an amused, knowing manner.

There was a wicked glint in his dark jade eyes. "Cooking is squaw's work, isn't it?"

Leah smiled and shook her head, silently amazed that they could be joking about the Indian blood that flowed in his veins after she had made that challenging and unwittingly derogatory remark last night.

"I've heard that it is," she admitted.

"Will the pan do, then?" He held it out for her inspection.

"I think so." Leah took the pan and set it on the ground beside her. "Hand me the canteen, will you? I'll start mixing the stew while you get the fire hot."

First, Leah rinsed out the makeshift pan with a little water, wiping it dry with some tissue. By guess, she roughly measured the amount of water required into the pan and added the dried soup.

"What can I use to stir this?" She glanced at Reilly, her face breaking into a sudden smile. "Better yet, how are we going to eat this without a spoon?"

"Here's my pocket knife." He handed it to her with the blade closed. "I guess we'll have to stab the meat and potatoes with the blade and drink the liquid."

"The pan will have to work as a community bowl,

too, I guess," she laughed shortly, and stirred the dry ingredients into the water.

It was almost an hour later before Reilly could separate a few glowing coals from the fire bed to heat the stew. He propped the pan an inch above the embers on some flat rocks.

It wasn't long before the liquid started bubbling, emitting an appetizing aroma.

In the interim, Reilly had fashioned two shallow bowls from the metal fragments of the plane, explaining that the sides of the pan would be too hot to drink from. When the stew was heated through, he took the shirt Leah had draped over a bush and folded it to use as a potholder to remove the pan from the coals.

Carefully he poured part of the stew into the two bowls and handed Leah's to her. Leah refused his offer to use the knife, choosing to scoop out the chunky pieces with a cracker. Neither utensils were efficient, but both served their purpose.

"Cigarette?" Reilly offered when they had finished their meal, removing a pack from his shirt pocket and shaking out a filtered tip for her.

'Mmm, please. Leah accepted the cigarette, bending forward as he lit the end with the burning tip of a stick from the fire.

They smoked their cigarettes in a comfortable silence. Leah finished hers first, then tossing the butt into the glowing camp fire.

'I suppose I should clean the dishes," she sighed.

'Might as well," Reilly agreed. "We might have to

use them tonight." His comment drew her attention to the sky, empty of any search plane. "Sand will work better than water to clean."

Drawing her gaze away from the sky, Leah picked up the pan and poured in a small handful of sand. When it was scoured clean she rinsed away the grit with a little water and started on the shallow bowls. Reilly picked up the canteen and emptied it into the pan.

"Why did you do that?" she frowned.

"I'm going to refill the canteen from the basin. While I'm gone I want you to have water on hand to pour on the fire in case you see a search plane," he answered.

"But it will put the fire out," Leah protested.

"It will also make a lot of smoke which with luck the pilot would see and come to investigate," Reilly pointed out.

"I see." Dimples edged into her cheeks. "The old Indian smoke trick."

"Right," he winked, and started walking toward the slope.

She scoured the two bowls clean, rinsing them with a handful of water from the pot and wiping them dry with a tissue. With that done, she checked the clothes she had draped over the bushes and found that they were dry. She folded hers up and put them in her suitcase. Reilly's she stacked neatly on top of his suitcase. With only the partial use of her left hand, the task had taken some time, yet still Reilly hadn't returned. The sun was making its fiery presence in the sky felt. Leah added some more wood to the fire and sat down away from the blaze to wait.

Finally she saw him on the ledge above. He started down the fairly steep slope with the canteen in one hand and a four-foot-long board in the other.

"I wondered what was taking you so long," Leah called when he was half way down. "You made a sidetrip for more firewood."

At the base of the slope, Reilly made his reply. "No, I'm not going to use this board for firewood." He set the canteen beside the box of packaged food. "I'm going to try and split it in two and make lean-to poles out of it. It's going to get hotter and we'll need to get out of the sun."

After splitting the board down the middle with the pocket-knife as his wedge, he whittled each end to a point. The stiff, blanket-like sheet they had used last night had grommets in each corner. The stakes supported two of the blanket's corners and Reilly weighted the other two to the ground with rocks.

"A strong wind would probably blow it down, but it keeps out the sun," he declared, then bent down to sit inside his lean-to and waved Leah to join him.

She moved eagerly to its shade, revelling in the coolness after the burning rays of the sun. Reilly picked up one of the sticks from the firewood pile and began whittling on it with his knife.

"What are you making now?" she asked curiously.

"I thought I'd try my hand at carving a spoon."

Lying on her back with her arm as a pillow, she watched him shaving away the outer layer of wood with his knife. The steady rhythm of the slashing blade was slightly hypnotic. Soon she found her eyelids growing heavy.

"Why don't you take a siesta?" Reilly suggested when she tried to blink away the tiredness. "I'll keep a watch for any search planes."

"I think I will." She stopped fighting the drowiness and closed her eyes.

CHAPTER FOUR

Leah slept through the heat of the afternoon. The same rhythmic sound that lulled her to sleep was the first one she heard when she wakened. Reilly was sitting in the long shadow of the lean-to, whittling on a stick that now bore considerable resemblance to a wooden spoon.

Blinking the sleep from her eyes, she started to push herself into a sitting position. Unconsciously she used both arms as a lever and gasped sharply at the pain that stabbed like a burning knife in her left arm. Quickly she switched all her weight to her right arm.

"That was stupid," she muttered.

"Is your arm bothering you a lot?" Reilly's green eyes narrowed with piercing scrutiny.

"Only when I do something like that." She sat upright, cradling her left arm in her lap as the shooting pain began to recede. Her mouth felt scratchy and dry as if coated with wool. A frown marred her forehead as she glanced around the circle. "I need a drink. Where's the canteen?"

"In the shade behind you."

Leah had to shift slightly to reach it. Uncapping it, she took a long swallow. The water was warm but deliciously wet. The funny taste left her mouth.

"How are you getting on with the spoon?" At her question, Reilly's knife stopped its slashing as he held it up for her to see. "It looks like a spoon." The knife resumed its work. A fly buzzed noisily about her head, pulling Leah's gaze to the empty sky. "There hasn't been any sign of a search plane?"

"No." He didn't elaborate. After several minutes of silence, he set the spoon-shaped piece of wood on the ground, folded back the knife blade and slipped it into his pocket. "We'll need some more firewood for tonight. I won't be gone long."

As he started up the slope, Leah scooted from beneath the lean-to and stood up to scratch her legs, arching her back to ease the stiffness from lying on the hard ground. The action tipped her head back, and a black object in the sky overhead caught her eye.

A buzzard was slowly circling. Leah shuddered, bringing her gaze swiftly to earth to focus on the slide. She was glad that the rock and debris had buried the plane and Grady. The desert scavenger was wasting his time.

She didn't want to let her thoughts dwell on its menacing presence, so she turned toward the western horizon. Shielding her eyes from the glare of the late afternoon sky, she studied the empty blueness. There was not a speck of anything. Surely by now the rescue party would be widening their search grid, she thought.

Her parents had probably received the notification that she was missing—and her brother, too. Oh, Lonnie, what a rotten birthday present! Tears misted her eyes at the dispiriting thought of the agony her family was going through.

An explosive sound ripped the air. Her first reaction was that a car had backfired before she realized that the idea was ludicrous because there were no cars. It had to have been a gunshot.

In a flash of memory, she recalled the pistol Reilly carried in his waistband of his levis. What could he have been shooting at? A snake? Terror gripped her throat. This area was probably crawling with venomous rattlesnakes.

"What if he's been bitten?" The thought, uttered aloud, made it seem all the more possible.

Spinning, she raced toward the slope. Her widened hazel eyes scanned the rocky ledge where he had disappeared from sight.

"Reilly! Reilly!" she screamed.

His reply was instant, and calmly clear. "It's all right," he called.

A few seconds later he appeared at the rim of the ledge, tall and bronzed and cloaked with an air of competency. Her knees threatened to buckle under her at the sight of him. Perspiration plastered his white shirt against his muscular chest. His hair glistened blue-black in the sun.

"I heard a shot." Leah's voice trembled.

An arm raised to show a jackrabbit dangling lifeless from his hand. "Tonight's dinner," he explained offhandedly. "I'll be down as soon as I get the firewood."

Then he disappeared again. He had looked so compellingly masculine standing there, a fact Leah had noted before, but it had never struck as forcibly as it had a second ago. She suddenly began to wonder about the women in his life and whether there was a special one that belonged to him.

Remembering the strong arms that had held her in sleep last night and the hard length of his body lying beside hers, she realized she envied the woman, if there was one. As a lover, Reilly—She stopped, shaking her head wryly. Her thoughts were becoming decidedly intimate.

Turning away from the slope, she walked back to the clearing. She knelt beside the box of food supplies, forcing her mind to concentrate on the task of deciding what could be served with the rabbit Reilly had shot. Setting aside a dried vegetable pouch, she added a packet of peaches to the water left in the pan.

When Reilly came down the slope a few minutes later laden with an armload of wood, she was still stirring the peaches, trying to hasten their absorption of the water. It was difficult not to look at him with the new sensual awareness that she felt.

She did her best to ignore it, though. "I hope you

don't expect me to clean that rabbit. I wouldn't know the first thing about skinning it," she said, eyeing the limp animal distastefully.

"Then you can watch me," Reilly grinned crookedly.

"No, thanks." She turned quickly back to her peaches, catching the gleam of devilry that sparkled in his look. "You fix the rabbit and I'll take care of the rest of the dinner."

She kept her attention firmly riveted on her task. Blood didn't make her squeamish, but the sight of that small carcass being cleaned wasn't all that pleasant.

"When I heard the shot, I had visions of a rattlesnake attacking you," she said.

"It's too hot for them to be out. They come to hunt just before sunrise and shortly after sundown," Reilly explained. "Besides, rattlesnakes don't attack. They're relatively timid reptiles. The only time a person has to worry about them is if he's unwary enough to stumble on one."

"Remind me not to go wandering about, then," she said with mock seriousness.

Reilly chuckled quietly, a pleasant sound that Leah found she liked very much. Glancing surreptitiously at his chiselled features, so lean and powerful, there was a lot she liked about him.

Later, after their meal of roasted rabbit, they sat and watched the orange sun wavering above the horizon. The western sky was painted a brilliant scarlet orange, the distant mountain range set afire with its flaming light.

There was so much emptiness in the wilderness land Leah studied. It was as if she and Reilly were the only two people on the whole of the earth.

She stared unblinkingly at the sunset. "Do you think the search planes will find us tomorrow?"

"Possibly."

A thin thread of fear stretched over her nerves. She turned. "What if they don't find us, Reilly? What if we're stranded here forever?"

He held her gaze for a long moment, looking deep into her hazel eyes. Then he smiled faintly and shook his head. "We won't be. We'll get out of here."

"Of course," she sighed, silently chiding herself for giving in to that momentary twinge of fear.

The plane had crashed only twenty-four hours ago, hardly enough time to start panicking that they wouldn't be found. One day, her mind echoed; it seemed much longer than that.

Standing, Reilly added two more small logs to the dying fire and took down the lean-to so the stiff blanket could be used as a cover. While the dwindling sunlight still gave enough light to see, he smoothed away the top layer of stones where their bed would be.

With the departure of the sun, the air became instantly chilled. Leah moved closer to the small fire, staring into its flames. Its toasting warmth couldn't reach her back. When she started shivering Reilly suggested it was time they went to sleep. A blanket of stars was overhead as she curled against him.

The second day was longer than the first. A great part of the first day had been occupied recovering what they could from the plane, finding water, building a fire, improvising cooking utensils and erecting the lean-to. None of that needed to be done the second day and time rested heavily on Leah's mind.

The heat of the sun seemed more intense, the perspiration prickling her skin. All day long, her gaze restlessly searched the sky for the rescue plane. The inactivity of waiting scraped at her nerves, although Reilly's outward composure of stoic calm didn't seem affected by it.

Only once had she seen anything. Jumping to her feet, she had pointed excitedly to the flash of sunlight on metal wings. "There! It's a plane, isn't it?"

As he stood beside her, his piercing gaze had searched the sky until he, too, saw the slow-flying plane far in the distance. "Yes, it's a plane," he had agreed calmly.

"I'll let them know we're here." She had turned sharply to get the canteen to douse the fire and send up the smoke signal that would reveal their location.

Strong fingers curled around her wrist, halting her. "It's too far away now."

Leah had waited, her gaze riveted on the plane, praying fervently for it to fly toward them. But it had continued on its course southward, growing smaller until it had disappeared.

"It will come back," she had declared in a low voice to conceal her disappointment and the fraying edges of despair.

But it hadn't.

That night Leah slept badly. The hard ground couldn't provide a cushion for her aching muscles already stiffened by two previous nights on the uncomfortable bed. Reilly slept with infuriating ease, wakening only twice to reach from beneath the cover to add wood from a nearby stack to the fire.

Awakening from a fitful doze, Leah discovered it was morning. She groaned at her lack of restful sleep and laid her head back on Reilly's arm to stare disgustedly at the brilliant blue sky. Her left arm throbbed painfully. She shifted against him, trying to ease her arm into a more comfortable and less painful position.

As she twisted on to her side, her gaze focused on his face. She almost hated the way he was sleeping so calmly. The impulse rose to waken him and deny him of sleep as she had been. While she was seriously contemplating it, his sooty lashes lifted partially open, screening his eyes to a smoky jade color.

"Good morning," he said in a voice that was disgustingly refreshed and relaxed.

Irritation flashed in her eyes. "Is it?" she snapped, and tugged at the stiff edge of the blanket to free it of his hold. "I don't know what's particularly good about it."

When he released it, she hurled the cover aside and scrambled awkwardly to her feet. Smoothly he joined her with an ease that betrayed not a trace of a sore or protesting muscle or joint.

"You didn't sleep well." Amusement danced in his look.

"That's an understatement! But then you slept sound enough for both of us," she muttered sarcastically.

"I don't think so." Silent laughter edged his voice. "There was a wiggling in my bed all night."

She glared at him, scraping the tousled light brown hair away from her face. She was tired and cross and taking it out on Reilly. It was unfair, but she couldn't seem to stop herself.

"You're lucky it didn't bite you," she retorted.

She knelt beside her suitcase, rummaging through it to find a clean blouse to replace the rumpled one she wore. Silently she swore that if he laughed openly at her grouchy reply, she would throw something at him.

As if sensing the slender thread that held her temper in check, Reilly didn't enlarge on the subject. "Put some water on to boil so I can shave, will you?" It was more of an order than a question.

Leah reacted unconsciously to the tone. "Heat your own water!" Then she cursed silently for being so ill-tempered when it wasn't his fault she hadn't slept. Her guilty sideways look caught the sharp narrowing of his eyes. "Never mind," she grumbled, "I'll do it." But she couldn't seem to stop her tongue from tacking on, "After all, it is squaw's work, isn't it?"

The harsh line of his mouth warned her that she was pushing her luck. "Are you trying to start an argument?" Reilly demanded.

"No," Leah sighed irritatedly.

"Good." He pivoted and walked into the brush.

She scraped a few glowing coals from the fire and

added more wood to the rest. The pan of water was balanced on the four supporting rocks around the separated embers.

With that accomplished, she shrugged off her blouse, the gash in her left arm burning constantly. She carefully eased the clean yellow blouse over it. She was buttoning the last button when Reilly returned. Sliding a glance at the pot, Leah saw the water was steaming.

"Your water is hot," she told him somewhat coolly.

"Thanks," was his equally indifferent reply. With a handkerchief from his suitcase, he set the pot off the coals, then paused. "Would you like to wash first?"

Shaking her head negatively, Leah opened her cosmetic case and took out the bottle of cleansing lotion to clean her face. The mirror in the lid of her cosmetic case was turned at just the right angle so that she saw not only her reflection, but Reilly's too.

It was a curiously intimate experience to watch a man shave. Long, sun-browned fingers gripped the razor, its blade slicing through the foamy lather and one day's stubble of beard. Each stroke of the blade revealed more of the bronzed skin below his cheekbones and the strong line of his jaw until the handsomely chiselled features were fully exposed.

As he rinsed away the traces of lather, Leah voiced the thought that had just occurred to her. "I thought Indians didn't shave."

"They didn't." Reilly wiped the razor dry and replaced it in his suitcase. His voice was emotionless and distant. "They plucked out the hair on their faces." Leah winced at the thought. "Is your arm bothering you this morning?" he asked in the same tone.

"A bit," she shrugged with one shoulder, carefully favoring the burning wound in the other arm.

"Let me take a look at it." He started toward her.

"There's no need," Leah refused quickly and sharply. It was his aloofness that made her reject his suggestion, combined with the lingering crossness of a sleepless night. "It's sore mostly because it's healing."

Reilly hesitated thoughtfully. "We don't have much bandage left in the kit. I'd rather not change it for a couple of days if it isn't bothering you too much."

"I said it was just healing pains," she repeated.

"Very well." He accepted her explanation with a faint grimness. "I'm going to get some more firewood. Have something to eat while I'm gone."

"I'm not hungry."

"It might make you feel better," he replied tautly.

"Improve my disposition, you mean," Leah flashed at his suggestion of criticism. "Well, I'm not hungry."

A moment of tense silence followed her challenging statement.

"I realize you didn't sleep well last night," Reilly spoke in an ominously quiet voice, "but I suggest, Miss Talbot, that you stop taking your frustration out on me."

Miss Talbot, she thought with a dejected sigh as his long strides carried him toward the slope, not Leah any more. She deserved the set-down, she reminded herself, but it didn't make it any less cutting.

With light make-up applied and her long hair brushed to a silken shine, she slipped off her shoes and shook out the sand. Removing her socks, she grimaced at the sand and dirt that had collected between her toes and on the bottom of her feet. They felt hot and sweaty, too.

The pan of warm water sat invitingly near, flecks of shaving foam still floating on top. She hesitated for only a second. It would be foolish to put on a clean pair of socks without washing her feet.

Treading carefully over the rough ground on her bare feet, she retrieved the handkerchief Reilly had laid over a bush to dry. With it as a washcloth and the small bar of soap from her cosmetic case, she started washing her feet in the pan of water. She rinsed the soap away with water from the canteen and wiped her feet dry with the tail of the rumpled blouse she had taken off earlier. The dirtied water she dumped on the sand.

It was nearly as good as taking a bath, she thought contentedly. When they were rescued, she decided she was going to laze in a bathtub full of bubbles for an hour, or possibly more. She tugged on her clean socks and shook the sand out of her shoes a second time.

As she slipped on the first shoe, she heard a humming sound. She frowned, listening intently, trying to recognize the cause. She couldn't tell which direction the sound was coming from, yet it seemed to be growing louder.

Her eyes widened in recognition. It was the drone of an airplane engine. She looked immediately toward the western sky. It was unbelievably near their position and flying toward it. The breeze from the east must have carried the sound until it was nearly above her.

With an excited shout to Reilly, Leah grabbed for the canteen and dumped the water on the fire. Only a trickle came out, sizzling to a tiny puff of smoke as it touched the fire. She stared at the insignificant puff in disbelief.

".You fool!" she muttered. "Why did you use all that water to wash your feet?"

The roar of the plane's engine came from overhead. Wrenching her gaze away from the fire, she looked above her head. There was no indication that they had been seen as it flew onward to the east into the sun.

"Here we are!" she shouted, running after the plane's shadow and waving her arms frantically. "Here we are! Down here!"

Reilly came racing down the slope, a miniature avalanche of small rocks rolling before him. "Pour water on the fire!" he shouted.

Leah stopped. "There isn't any water. I used it all."

His expression hardened at her statement, but there was no comment on her stupidity. Without breaking stride, he hit the level ground at the bottom of the slope. He paused long enough to pick up the wrinkled red cloth that had been their blanket and tossed it to her.

"Wave that in the air!" he snapped out the order. "The aluminum side up!"

As she obeyed, she was conscious of Reilly kneeling beside her cosmetic case, but she was more aware of the plane flying away from them. Then Reilly was standing beside her, the rectangular mirror from the lid of her cosmetic case in his hand.

While she waved the blanket until she thought her arm would drop off, he wigwagged the mirror in the sun, trying to pinpoint the flashing light on the plane. But the plane never wavered from its course.

"Come back!" Leah screamed. Her arm hung limply at her side, without the strength to raise the blanket one more time, her injured left arm cradled across her waist.

It disappeared into the sun. A tear slipped from her lashes, then another and another until there was a silent, steady stream down her cheeks. Her lips were salty with the taste of her tears.

"They didn't see us," she whispered in a choked, tight voice.

Her chin trembled as she turned to look at Reilly. His hands were on his hips in a stance of angry disgust. He was staring into the emptiness where the plane had been. He turned, turbulent green eyes briefly meeting hers before he walked back to the fire.

"I'm sorry, Reilly." Leah followed him. The stiff blanket was still clutched in her fingers, trailing along the ground behind her. "It's all my fault. I'd used all the water to wash my feet and I threw it away without thinking."

"Your feet?" he repeated dryly, his speaking glance saying all the things he didn't put into words.

"They were dirty," she offered lamely in defence.

Reilly began stacking the few remaining logs on to the fire. His silence was more crushing than any verbal condemnation. Finally Leah couldn't take it any more, and her anger and hurt erupted like a volcano.

"Why don't you say something?" she accused. "Why don't you shout at me and tell me what a stupid idiotic thing it was to do? We both know it was, so why don't you say it! Get angry or something! Don't just keep putting wood on the fire as if nothing had happened!"

"There wouldn't be any point," Reilly answered calmly, rising to his feet and brushing his hands on his thighs. Except for the grim tightness of his mouth an impersonal mask had slipped over his face. "I'm going to go and fill the canteen and bring down the firewood."

A broken sigh of frustration slipped from her constricting throat.

"What if the plane comes back while you're gone?"

"Wave the blanket and yell for me."

When he had disappeared up the slope, Leah collapsed on her knees. Her fingers relaxed their death grip on the blanket and it lay beside her, the shiny aluminum side catching the sun's rays. She was exhausted and emotionally drained.

She wanted to bury her head in her arms and cry silently at her stupidity, but she didn't dare. There was a chance that the plane might fly back this way. She couldn't risk being caught unaware a second time.

Sniffing back the tears, she wiped the salty dampness from her cheeks and started scanning the skies. Her ears strained to hear the drone of an airplane engine. There was only the desert mountain silence until the rolling of stones down the slope heralded Reilly's return.

After setting the armload of wood on the ground a few feet away from the fire, Reilly handed the canteen to Leah. "Have a drink."

She looked at it as if it were poison. She was hot and tired and very thirsty, but no matter how parched her throat might be, she didn't want to drink the water that might get them rescued.

"No," she refused with quiet firmness.

Exasperation straightened the line of his mouth. "A swallow isn't going to do any harm. Take a drink," he ordered.

Reluctantly Leah obeyed, taking a small sip and letting it roll around to wet her dry mouth before swallowing it. Moistening her lips with her tongue, she handed the canteen back to him, aware of the alert greenness of his eyes watching her, but unable to meet it.

The canteen was set in the shade of the firewood. Without a word Reilly walked over and picked up the thin blanket lying on the ground beside Leah. She frowned, wondering what he intended to do with it, then saw him erecting the lean-to.

Her frown deepened. "Won't we need the blanket to signal the plane?"

Reilly didn't turn away from his task as he answered. "It can be torn down in seconds if we see the plane. In the meantime it will be of more service as a sunshade."

Leah stared at the crackling fire. It burned cleanly, a thin wisp of smoke rising and disappearing in the clear desert air almost immediately. Shimmering heat waves danced above the fire.

"The plane flew almost directly over us," she said quietly. "I didn't hear it coming until it was almost here. Why couldn't they see us?"

"In the first place," Reilly secured the last corner of the lean-to, "they were flying into the morning sun. Their vision was impaired. And in the second place, they were looking for airplane wreckage." His head nodded in the general direction of the slide. "Ours is buried beneath that."

"They would have seen the smoke signal, though," she sighed, gazing into the morning sky. "It's my fault."

"Stop feeling sorry for yourself," Reilly ordered firmly.

"I'm not!" Leah protested indignantly.

"Yes, you are, and it's not going to change anything."

"I never said it would," she retorted.

"Then let's stop discussing what happened and be prepared in case the plane flies back this way."

Leah paused. Something in his voice made her ask, "Do you think it will?"

"I don't know." Nothing in his expression revealed what Reilly really thought or believed.

CHAPTER FIVE

A cloud blocked out the western sun. A halo of gold formed around its gray-white shape, then streamed to earth to bronze the sage-covered ground.

Leah's blouse was damp with perspiration, clinging to her like a second skin. Her arm ached with an agonizing throb. That morning's exertion when she had tried and failed to use it to wave the blanket at the plane had increased its soreness.

Wearily she pressed her right hand against her forehead for a few seconds, then lifted her head, her hand pushing the hair away from her face. All day they had waited and the plane had not returned. It was nearing sundown.

Her clouded hazel eyes moved to Reilly, relentlessly watching the sky yet seeming to be miles away in thought. "How long do you think they'll continue looking for us?'' She voiced the fear that had been recurring all day.

The remoteness remained in his bland jade eyes as he glanced at her. "It's hard to say. An extensive air search is expensive and time-consuming," he replied. "They'll probably look for a couple more days at most. After that, they'll ask local pilots to keep a lookout for any sign of wreckage and send out one or two search planes of their own."

The knowledge was sobering. The possibility of being stranded in this wilderness for more days seemed probable. Leah knew she couldn't think about that without sinking into a morass of guilt feelings. And Reilly was right, that wouldn't solve anything.

"I think I'll get us something to eat," she murmured.

Food didn't interest her. At lunch, she had chewed indifferently on a stack of beef jerky, knowing that she had to eat something. It was the latter motivation instead of hunger that prompted her to cook the evening meal. The side benefit would be taking her mind off their situation.

After three days, the choice of dried food dishes had dwindled considerably. Leah glanced through the few that remained, searching for one that at least sounded appetizing.

Out of the corner of her eye, she saw Reilly crouching in front of the suitcases. Curious, she shifted slightly to see what he was doing, and her lips parted in surprise. It was her suitcase he had opened and was searching through the contents.

"What do you think you're doing, going through my suitcase?" she challenged, rising angrily to her feet and striding to his side. He didn't even look up. "Those happen to be my personal things and you have no right going through them!"

He set a stack of her lingerie to one side and started going through her assortment of outer clothes. She tried taking them out of his hands to jam them back in her suitcase, but he picked them up and discarded them quicker than she could stop him.

"Did you hear what I said?" she demanded finally.

"I'm not stealing anything," Reilly answered her finally. "I'm trying to find if you have anything suitable for walking."

"You could ask!" Leah retorted bitterly. She tried to fold the items he had discarded. "You don't have to rummage through my things!"

"I've seen women's clothes before. There's no need to let your modesty embarrass you." He held up a pair of corded slacks of wheat tan and a long-sleeved blouse of white with tiny gold and brown diamond patterns crisscrossing it. "These should do."

Leah sat back on her heels, staring at his impassive face bewilderedly. "Should do for what?" she frowned. A piece of his earlier remark came filtering back. "What did you mean 'suitable for walking?' "

"We're leaving," Reilly announced calmly, and turned to her cosmetic case. "Do you have any face cream in here?" he asked as he snapped open the lid.

"Yes." She reached in and picked up the jar. "Why do you want it?" The answer to that wasn't nearly so important when his announcement sank in. "How are we leaving?"

"On foot, of course." He flicked a brief glance at her, then opened the jar and removed a dab of cream with his forefinger, rubbing it experimentally between his finger and thumb. "This cream is going to protect your pale face from the sun."

"On foot? You must be crazy!" Leah stared out over the vast desert mountain wilderness.

"It would be crazier to stay here." The cosmetic case was abandoned as Reilly opened his own suitcase.

"I know you think I'm stupid—" Leah began hotly.

"I think nothing of the sort," Reilly interrupted evenly.

"But I do know," she continued with barely a break, "that when you're lost and people are looking for you, you're supposed to stay in one place and not go wandering off. We don't even know where we are!"

He removed two of his dirty shirts from the suitcase and closed the lid. "I have a rough idea."

"Wonderful," Leah murmured sarcastically. When he rose to his feet she followed as closely as his shadow. "Does that mean we're somewhere in Nevada? I could have made that guess."

Reilly stopped shortly, nearly causing her to run into his broad back. His gaze was hard as steel when he looked at her.

"We're on the east side of the Monitor Range, which would put us roughly sixty miles from the nearest town as the crow flies. In this terrain, on foot, it would probably be ninety miles.''

In this emptiness, it seemed impossible that they were even that close to civilization. ''We could die out there,'' Leah argued.

''We could die here,'' he pointed out.

''Yes, but''—his reply put her off her stride for a second—''here, we at least have a chance of being found, of signalling the next plane.''

''When will it come, Leah?'' Reilly studied her rebellious yet frightened expression. ''Tomorrow? The day after? Three days from now? When?''

''I don't know.'' Her hand lifted to wave the question aside. ''But it will come. My parents and Lonnie won't stop looking until they find me. I know they won't!''

''I agree, but time is still the factor.''

''Why?'' she demanded.

''Because in three, maybe four more days we won't have the food, the water, or the strength to walk out of here.'' The lowness of his voice, his calmness, seemed designed to impress on her the gravity of their situation.

Wildly, she looked up the slope in the direction where he had said he had found the water. ''But—''

''The water I found in the rock basin is drying up,'' Reilly explained. ''It's evaporating in this heat.''

Foolishly Leah had regarded their water supply as inexhaustible. She had forgotten Reilly's comment that water was invaluable in desert terrain.

A tide of helplessness washed over her. "You should have told me."

"Perhaps." Reilly adopted the same indifferent attitude about discussing what had already been done as he had when Leah had used all the water to wash her feet. What had been done was done, and as far as he was concerned, there was no purpose in rehashing the reason.

"If we tried to walk for help," Leah still didn't endorse the idea despite the logic of Reilly's reasons, "how would we know which way to go?"

"We'll go south."

"Why?" she persisted stubbornly. "Why not west? When we flew off course, we came east. Surely we should go back that way."

Reilly breathed in deeply, as if his patience with her questions was thinning. "The mountain ranges run in a north-south line. I don't know how many of them we would have to cross before we reached either a highway or a town. Finding a safe way over them and down would take too much time. That same reason rules out going east. To the north, I can see mountains. If we went that way, we would have to travel along the ridge. But south, we have a valley. The walking will be easier and we can make better time."

"We could also get lost," Leah point out.

"I won't get lost," he assured her dryly.

His confidence irritated her. He was absolutely positive he was right. With all of her arguments dismissed, she retaliated with lashing sarcasm.

"How stupid of me to forget that you're part

Indian," she inserted cuttingly. "Of course you wouldn't get lost."

His carved features darkened ominously. "You're quite right."

She pressed her lips together. Her barb had somehow fallen short of its mark. Exhaling an angry breath, she glanced away.

"I don't care what you think," she muttered. "I don't think we should leave here. The search plane could find us any time."

"We're leaving in the morning at first light," Reilly stated calmly.

Leah tossed her head back defiantly meeting his cool gaze. "You can leave if you want. I'm staying here."

"No, you are not." His jaw tightened.

"And how are you going to stop me?" she asked pertly. "I somehow don't think you're strong enough to carry me all the way and I'm certainly not going to go with you willingly. That puts us at something of an impasse, doesn't it? I won't go and you won't leave without me, so that means we'll stay here."

"You're making a mistake." His eyes had narrowed into a lazy, measuring look.

"I don't think so." This time it was she who brimmed with self-confidence.

"All right," he nodded curtly in acceptance. "You can stay here. I'll leave in the morning."

Here eyes widened in amazement. "What?"

"It's probably the best solution anyway. I can make better time without you along and you can be here to signal the plane in case it flies back over this area again. If it doesn't, then within three day's time, at the outside, I shall have reached help and be able to send someone back for you," Reilly concluded, satisfaction gleaming in his eyes.

"You mean you'd leave me—here—alone?" Leah repeated in disbelief.

"It's the logical thing to do. This way we can cover both possibilities for obtaining help." He paused, as if studying the idea more thoroughly. "I'll have to take the canteen with me, but you can use the pan to fetch water. You can keep the dried food with you since I won't have a water supply to depend on. I'll take the beef jerky, though."

"No!"

A black eyebrow shot up in surprise at her vigorous protest, a studied arrogance in the action. "I shall need some food," Reilly commented dryly.

"I don't care about that," Leah frowned. "You aren't honestly going to leave me?"

"Why not?" He tipped his head to one side. "Are you going with me?"

"No."

"Then you must be staying here," he shrugged, and turned away.

Her fingers closed over the hard flesh of his arm, halting him when he would have walked away from her. She stared into his impassive face, lean and compellingly handsome in its proud, carved lines.

"You really would leave me here by myself, wouldn't you?" Leah murmured.

A faintly bemused smile crooked his mouth as if he didn't understand why she had doubted it. "Yes," Reilly answered simply.

"Well, you're sadly mistaken if you think you're going to leave me here alone while you go traipsing off," she vowed. "If you go, then I'm going too."

"But you were going to stay here to signal the plane," he reminded her with a wry shake of his head.

"I'm going with you," Leah stated emphatically. "I don't care how practical it is. You can't make me stay here."

The instant the last sentence was spoken, her teeth bit into her lip in angry memory. Only minutes ago she had been insisting that he couldn't make her go with him in the morning.

"In that case," Reilly drawled, "I guess you'll leave with me."

As he started to turn away, Leah caught the roguish glint in his eyes. "You tricked me," she hissed accusingly. "You never intended to leave me here by myself!"

He paused, an eyebrow raising in a complacent arch, glittering eyes dancing over his face. "Did you really think I would leave my squaw behind?" he mocked with decided jest.

She released his arm, and the open palm of her hand swung in an arc toward the deepening grooves beside his mouth. Reilly didn't attempt to check her slapping swing. He simply drew back so that she missed her target.

When her hand had swished by, he captured her

wrist in his fingers, smiling openly at her burst of temper. Leah tried to twist free of his steel grip. Her left arm was throbbing too painfully to be of any help.

He held her easily. Her angry struggles only brought her closer to the firmness of his chest. A throaty chuckle rolled from his lips.

"I don't think it's funny!" Leah tossed back her head to glare at him coldly.

The amusement faded from his gaze as he stared down at her. The brilliant fire that leaped into his eyes dazzled her, halting her attempts to pull free. Her heart skipped a beat when his attention shifted lazily to her mouth.

His thumb slowly rubbed the inside of her wrist. His other hand came up to absently smooth the hair from her face. It stayed to cup the back of her neck. A shiver of anticipation raced up her spine. She was already swaying toward him when his hand exerted pressure to draw her lips to his.

His mouth closed over hers warmly, masterfully firm in its possession. Her muscles melted closer to the lean hardness of his tapering length. His kiss ignited a slow-burning flame in her midsection that languidly trailed through her limbs.

Yet when the moment came for the embrace to deepen with passion, Reilly relaxed the pressure at the back of her neck that had drawn her on tiptoe to him. Weakened by his kiss, her legs couldn't support her in that precarious stance and lowered her away from the male lips.

The gold tips of her lashes fluttered partially open.

Through their veil, she gazed unsteadily at him. Her breath was coming in uneven spurts. The look in his eyes was gentle and friendly yet seemingly masked.

"We're in this together all the way, Leah," Reilly said quietly. "We both leave in the morning."

"Yes," she nodded.

His hand uncurled from her neck, a finger trailing lightly over her cheek as he smiled, forming crinkling lines at the corners of his eyes. Leah couldn't help wondering if the kiss had been a means of persuading her to agree without more arguments.

Reilly moved a step away, reaching into the pocket of his shirt and taking out the pack of filtered cigarettes. He shook two out and lit them one at a time.

He handed one to Leah. "Shall we smoke the peacepipe?" A smile played with his mouth.

"Why not?" she smiled, and shook her head wryly, wishing she felt as normal and unmoved by the kiss as he did.

There was the barest tremor in her hand when she accepted the lit cigarette to betray the shaken state of her senses. Her lips still felt the warm imprint of his mouth as she inhaled deeply on the filtered end.

It was a good thing, she decided, that they were leaving in the morning. She was definitely attracted to Reilly physically. More days alone in their isolated camp and a few more expert kisses might increase the temptation of night. At least the exhaustion of the trail would dull her awareness of her virilely masculine companion.

A gauzy cloud drifted between them from Reilly's cigarette. "When we've finished smoking," he said idly, "you can go ahead with your dinner preparations while I organize what we'll need to take with us tomorrow."

The remaining daylight hours were filled with activity. The three-quarter moon had barely risen when Reilly announced that they should go to sleep early to rest up for the long walk ahead of them.

In his arms beneath the blanket, Leah felt the stirring of her pulse in response to the male length of him molded against her. Since the afternoon's kiss, she had expected him to attempt to make love to her tonight.

Expected was the wrong word. She had anticipated that he would make love to her, and with dangerous honesty, she admitted that she had been partly looking forward to it. The even rise and fall of his chest beneath her head was disappointing.

What manner of man was Reilly Smith, she asked herself? She knew she was an attractive woman, yet in three days he had kissed her once. Even then, although it had been an ardent kiss, it hadn't been exactly passionate.

Other men that she had dated would have quickly tried to take advantage of this situation she and Reilly were in—thrown together constantly by the isolation, forced to sleep together to endure the cold mountain desert night. Not that she had dated a lot of lecherous men. It was just that, under these circumstances, it would be easy for a man to take advantage of her.

Yet Reilly hadn't. It certainly wasn't because he lacked experience—the mastery of his kiss this afternoon wouldn't support that theory. When they had first met in the waiting lounge of the flying service, there had been admiration in his eyes when he looked at her.

Her own response to his kiss had indicated that she was not indifferent to him. So why hadn't he pursued her unwritten invitation?

Leah sighed angrily and shifted her throbbing left arm to lie across the muscular flatness of his stomach. She was being ridiculously feminine. She should be glad that she wasn't having to fight off his advances every second instead of wishing he would make one.

Forcing her lashes to close, Leah ordered herself to go to sleep. After last night's fitful dozing, she drifted off almost instantly.

Strong fingers pushed the hair away from her temples. "It's time to wake up," the male voice spoke insistently.

The cover was pulled away from their heads. Leah shivered at the intruding cold and tried to snuggle deeper into the curve of Reilly's shoulder. The same fingers curved under her chin.

"I said it's time to wake up," Reilly repeated with indulgent humor.

Moaning in protest, she peered through her lashes at the outside world. Except for the crackling fire, there was utter silence. Overhead sparkled the brightest stars Leah ever remembered seeing, thousands of them glittering with profound brilliance against a curtain of black.

"It's still dark," she grumbled.

"It won't be for long. Come on." His arm tightened around her side, drawing her up in a sitting position as he pushed himself up.

"We're honestly getting up at this hour?" Leah protested, barely stifling a yawn.

"It's nearly daybreak. You'd better get the water boiling so we can have what's left of that instant oatmeal," he ordered, pushing her the rest of the way out of the bed.

"Who's hungry?" she muttered.

"You will be when we start down the mountain if you don't eat something now."

Leah admitted silently that he was probably right, but she wasn't interested in food. What she really wanted was another couple of hours' sleep. Instead she poured water from the canteen into the metal pan and balanced it on the rocks beside the fire to boil.

The lonely wail of a faraway coyote echoed through the stillness. Leah huddled closer to the small fire, seeking its warmth. The eerie call drew her gaze to the landscape. The three-quarter moon frosted the ground with a silvery glow.

A ribbon of bubbles started to form in the pan of water, forcing her to leave the fire's circle for the oatmeal, bowls, and the two carved wooden spoons. A glance at Reilly saw him folding their stiff blanket into a small square, adding it to the other small items they would backpack with them.

When the water boiled, Leah stirred the oatmeal into it. It was difficult to gauge how much water was needed without a measuring cup, but this morning the oatmeal was neither lumpy nor runny. With the last portion, she had found the right mixture.

"Breakfast is ready," she called softly, spooning some into her bowl and giving Reilly the largest amount.

While they ate, a pink hue touched the eastern horizon as dawn began its silent appearance. The coppery pink pushed back the night, making way for a golden haze. By the time Leah had cleaned their dishes with sand, the entire sky was bathed in the half-light of sunrise.

Reilly handed her the canteen. "Drink all the water you can hold, then I'll go and fill it up."

After several swallows, she paused. "What are we going to do for water along the way? This canteen doesn't hold that much."

"We'll have to count on finding it." He waited for her to take another drink. "If there's water on the desert floor, it will probably be along the base of the mountains. Once we get down into the valley, we'll stay close to them."

After drinking as much as she could, she handed the canteen to him. While he disappeared up the slope, she changed into the clothes he had deemed suitable for the long walk. She was tucking in the tail of her blouse when he returned.

His green eyes swiftly appraised her appearance. "You don't have a hat, do you?" His mouth tightened grimly when she shook her head negatively. "A scarf?"

"Yes." She rummaged through her suitcase until she found the gold and brown silk scarf and held it up for him to see.

Reilly studied it for a considering moment. "It will have to do. Tie it around your head like a turban. At least it will protect your head from the sun."

Leah did as she was told. It was difficult with the searing pain in her arm. "I don't see what good it will do," she protested.

"If you'd ever had your scalp sunburned, you wouldn't say that," he replied dryly.

"What about your head?" She glanced at him pointedly, only to find he was tying a blue bandana around his jet-dark hair.

His was done more swiftly and more expertly than hers. When he had finished, Leah could see the inherent traces of his Indian ancestry. The inborn stamp of ruthless nobility was more striking than before.

He opened the jar of cold cream and offered it to her. "Put it on thick," he ordered.

"Why?" Leah frowned and scooped out a generous amount.

"To protect your face from the sun," he answered patiently, and did the same.

The white cream looked strange against his sunbrowned skin. "Since when did Indians need protection from the sun?" she teased.

"Everyone needs protection from the sun," Reilly

grinned, "including Indians. One tribe of Plains Indians used to rub sunflower oil all over their bodies for that purpose." He watched Leah smear the cream over her face. "Your nose is already a little red. I'd leave a coating of cream on it for extra protection."

His carved features glistened like a bronzed statue in the soft morning light. There was nothing to wipe the excess cream from her hands, so Leah followed his suit and used her trouser legs.

"There isn't anything more you need out of the suitcase, is there?" Reilly questioned.

"No."

"I'm going to set them over by the rock slide, then we'll get loaded up."

While he walked to the slide area where the plane was buried, Leah carefully touched the area around the wound on her left arm. It was burning as if a hot knife was being held against it and sore nearly down to her elbow. Yet it didn't feel as if her arm was swollen. She wondered if she should ask Reilly to take a look at it.

His cautioning comment of yesterday morning that they didn't have much bandage left and his desire for an early start on the trail while it was still cool made her decide not to bother him. The wound was obviously healing, and it had been an ugly gash.

"Are you ready to load up?" His long supple strides had carried him back into the clearing, his gaze touching her briefly.

"Why not?" Leah shrugged.

He had fashioned two crude shoulder packs out of

his shirts. The lighter one, containing the blanket and cooking utensils, he tied on her back. The heavier and more cumbersome one with the first-aid kit, food box, and flashlight, Reilly fastened on himself.

"Here." He handed her one of the sticks that had been used to support the lean-to.

"What's this for?" she frowned. "To chase the snakes out of my path?"

"It's a walking stick. It'll come in handy on some of the steeper stretches of the mountain." He walked over to the fire and stirred the ashes with the other stick, covering the remains with gravel and sand. "Are you ready?" he asked.

"I guess so." She shifted the pack on her shoulders to a more comfortable position, then laughed. "I feel like a squaw carrying a papoose on her back."

Reilly laughed softly, a dark glint in his jade eyes that was oddly disturbing. "Then let's hit the trail, squaw woman."

Waving her stick, Leah motioned for him to lead the way. Reilly started off, setting an easy pace, but one that could be maintained.

The level ridgetop gave way to the sloping mountainside. A lean jackrabbit darted swiftly out of their path while a lizard sunning himself on a rock stuck out his tongue as they passed. The sun was a yellow sphere above the horizon.

CHAPTER SIX

Rivulets of perspiration ran down her neck to the hollow between her breasts. The straps of the crude backpack chafed at her shoulders, adding to her discomfort.

The blazing sun was nearing its noonday notch, the fiery rays beat relentlessly down. Leaning heavily on her stick, Leah paused, winded, to catch her breath. The backs of her legs achingly protested the sight of the downhill grade still before them. All morning long they had zigzagged down the mountain and there was farther yet to go.

"How much farther is it, for heaven's sake?" Leah cried in a tone of exasperated anger.

Reilly halted several yards ahead, squinting his eyes against the sun to look back at her. "Distances are deceiving in open country." He wiped the sweat from around his mouth with the back of his hand.

"You're telling me," she muttered.

"Do you want to rest here or wait until we get to the bottom?"

When will that be—next year? Leah wondered tiredly. "How long has it been since we stopped last?" Since starting down the mountain, they had stopped every hour for a ten-minute rest.

"About twenty minutes ago," Reilly answered.

It seemed like a year, but Leah gritted her teeth and pushed onward with her stick. "Let's go down."

She wondered why they didn't just sit on their rumps and slide down to the bottom. The grade was certainly steep enough, but Reilly maintained his zigzag course, doubling the distance while lessening the severe downhill strain.

Her left arm was hurting her more now. Its weight swinging freely at her side seemed to increase the pull on the knitting wound. She tucked her left hand in the waistband of her slacks to form a natural sling. It helped, although it made balancing on the rockier stretches awkward.

Both shoes were rubbing against her heels. Leah knew she would soon have blisters to contend with. She lifted the pack on her back, but it slid back to the already chafed area. So she trudged on, putting one aching foot in front of the other.

Except for an occasional glance to be sure Reilly was still ahead of her, she concentrated on only the ground ahead of her feet. She tried to blank out all her aches and pains and the dryness of her mouth and throat.

Time became meaningless. Leah didn't know if she had walked for an hour or four hours when the ground finally levelled out beneath her feet. Reilly was already shedding his pack.

"We'll rest here for a couple of hours and stay out of the worst of the heat," he announced.

If she had had the energy, Leah would have cheered. Instead she sank to her knees, shrugging the chafing pack off her right arm and gently easing it off her throbbing left.

Dully she watched Reilly take a quick swallow from the canteen before handing it to her. The sound of the water sloshing against the sides was beautiful. She was so thirsty she knew she could drink it dry. But her thirst reminded her how precious water was and she settled for a swallow.

Opening her pack, Reilly removed the blanket and picked up the stick she had dropped on the ground. He looked disgustingly fresh, she thought, as if he could walk down ten such mountains without drawing a labored breath.

"Why don't you look as tired as I feel?" she sighed as he swiftly set up the lean-to.

He smiled faintly. "Probably because I don't spend five days a week behind a desk." The last corner of the lean-to was secured. "Come on, get out of the sun."

Leah willingly crawled into the shade, stretching out on her back. Her only wish was to never move again. Then Reilly was bending over her, his green eyes mocking and gently amused.

"Here, gnaw on this for a while." A stick of beef jerky was in his hand.

"I haven't the strength to eat anything." She waved it aside with a flick of her fingers.

"Eat!" It was an order not to be disobeyed as he placed the meat stick between her parted lips.

Reluctantly she obeyed, knowing he stubbornly wouldn't leave her alone until she did. Her jaws were weary from chewing by the time she had finished. Sighing, she closed her eyes to rest and was almost instantly asleep.

A hand shook her shoulder. She forced her eyes open to focus on Reilly, squatting beside her on the right. The pack was again strapped to his back, the canteen in his hand.

"It's time we left. Have a drink while I repack," he offered.

Leah pushed herself up, fighting the blackness that swirled sickeningly in front of her eyes. She took a hesitant sip of water and handed the canteen back. While Reilly started taking down the lean-to around her, she pressed a hand to her burning forehead and waited for the dizziness to subside.

I feel awful, she thought to herself.

Her left arm felt like a balloon, but she inwardly shrugged that thought away as the cause of her nausea. There wasn't a part of her body that didn't ache.

The sun had begun its westward trek, but the heat,

even in the shade, was scorching. If anything was to
blame, she decided it was the feverish heat and her
general exhaustion. She moved slowly to her feet, not
wanting any quick movement to bring the dizziness
back.

Reilly had the blanket back in her pack and ready
to strap on. While he was adjusting it in place on her
back, he accidentally brushed the area near her
wound. Leah winced at the knife-sharp pain.

"Does it hurt?" he asked instantly, his alert gaze
missing nothing.

"Everything hurts," she grimaced.

He handed her the walking stick. "Are you ready to
go on?"

At her brief nod, Reilly took the lead. Although he
set the same slow pace as before, Leah had trouble
keeping up. At each step, pain jarred through her
body. Twice he had to wait for her to catch up.

The rays of the sun seemed to set her skin on fire,
burning through her clothes until she felt drowned in
a river of perspiration. Waves of weakness kept
eroding her strength. Her parched throat made
swallowing difficult.

The ten-minute rest break at the end of the first
hour was all too short. The one swallow of water
hadn't begun to quench her thirst and her throat felt
as dry as the desert sand. Her mind cried that she
couldn't go any farther, but with feverish determination, she pushed herself up.

In memory, she could hear her brother Lonnie
chiding, "I told you girls couldn't keep up." His voice

sounded so clearly in her mind that she had to brush a hand in front of her glazed eyes to keep his image from dancing before her.

At Reilly's concerned look, she smiled tiredly. "I'm all right," she said hoarsely, more to convince herself than him.

"Hold this pebble in your mouth," he instructed as he handed the small stone to her. "It will keep the saliva working and help your thirst."

It did help to moisten her mouth as they started out again. Leah tried hard to follow the path Reilly was taking, but she kept weaving from one side to the other. The fire raging inside kept feeding her growing weakness. She tried focusing her gaze on Reilly, using his broad shoulders as a lifeline to draw her onward. The world was spinning before her eyes and she kept losing sight of him in the intermittent moments of reeling blackness. She could feel herself beginning to lose consciousness and was terrified.

"Reilly!" Her cry for help was a croaking whisper, made thicker by the pebble in her mouth. She stumbled and leaned heavily on the stick to regain her balance. Before her reeling senses collapsed under the raging heat and unquenchable thirst, she called to him desperately again. "Reilly."

Then she had no more strength. Her knees started to buckle beneath her and only the stick was keeping her upright. As she fought to keep the blackness away, she sobbed because she didn't think he had heard her. She had fallen so far behind.

The stick wavered in its support and she began to

sink slowly to the ground. A pair of strong arms circled her waist, easing her down gently.

"Reilly," she breathed, unable to see him clearly yet recognizing the feel of those arms that had held her in sleep these last nights. "I'm sorry, I can't make it any farther."

"Don't talk," was his low reply. He propped her against his chest.

The canteen was held to her lips, but most of the water trickled down her chin when she couldn't make her mouth swallow the precious liquid. He started to brush the damp tendrils of hair from her face, then stopped abruptly, his rough hand cupped on her cheek.

"My God, you're burning up with fever," Reilly muttered.

Quickly he stripped the pack from her back and unbuttoned her blouse. The pain was excruciating when he started to pull the sleeve back from her wound. Leah cried out sharply, sickening blackness swirling more thickly in front of her.

Through it, she heard the angry hiss of his breath. "You crazy woman!" he snarled. "Why the hell didn't you tell me how much this was hurting?"

Her tongue moved heavily to reply. "It's healing."

"Healing? Like hell—it's infected!"

With a groan of defeat, Leah surrendered to the threatening blackness, letting it carry her away to oblivion. The sensation followed that she was floating above the ground, cradled against Reilly's chest by a pair of strong arms. Her consciousness returned long enough for her to realize that Reilly was carrying her before she drifted away again.

A beautiful dream world closed around her. She was lying beside a mirror-smooth pool of clear water where green grass grew thickly along its banks. Overhead the branches of willow trees veiled the scarlet fire of a setting sun. Their leaves were green, a more brilliant green than the jade color of Reilly's eyes. A blessed coolness bathed her burning forehead. A trace of woodsmoke was in the air.

Then she was being lifted and her blouse removed. She moaned a protest at the interruption of her serenely peaceful vision.

"Hold as still as you can," was Reilly's gentle request.

Her lashes fluttered open, her eyes focusing on his jet dark head framed by a willow bough. "I'm having the most wonderful dream," she murmured. "There are trees and water and grass."

"It isn't a dream," Reilly told her as he removed the bandage from her arm and began washing the infected wound. "Evidently a Basque shepherd has at some time partially dammed a small spring to water his sheep."

It was real, she sighed to herself, and drifted again into unconsciousness.

The green world vanished, and she was stumbling over sun-scorched earth. The fiery rays of the sun blinded her eyes and burned her skin, its relentless blaze never once slackening.

At intervals, the coolness of water touched her

parched lips. Sometimes it was Lonnie holding the canteen to her mouth, teasing her as he had done when they were children when her short legs were unable to keep up with his long, lanky strides.

Other times it was Reilly telling her to lie still and rest. He couldn't seem to understand that she was condemned to walking beneath the searing sun. So she kept walking, surrounded by a furnace of heat.

The rising of the moon brought no relief. Its silvery glow burned white-hot from the sky. The desert night did not cool as it had always done. Perspiration boiled on her skin.

The sun was worst. Leah cried aloud when it returned to the sky, yet there was no escape from its fierce temperature. The only protection she had to prevent her from being consumed by the flaming tongues was her clothes. To her terror, she felt them being removed and struggled wildly to stop it.

"Leah, can you hear me?" Reilly's firm voice pierced her nightmare world.

"Yes." She sobbed with relief that she hadn't been abandoned. Her glazed eyes opened to discover that she was again in the green oasis, Reilly bending beside her, stripped to the waist.

His compelling gaze wouldn't let her slip back into the blackness. "I have to take off your clothes." Each word was spoken slowly and distinctly so that Leah would understand despite her delirium.

Her head lolled to one side in an effort to protest. She couldn't let him see her naked. It was against every moral principle her parents had instilled.

"No, you mustn't," she pleaded in a fever-choked whisper.

"Listen to me." His voice was low and insistent. "There's no need for you to be ashamed and embarrassed that I'll be seeing you unclothed. An Indian does not look at a naked body as a form to be sexually glorified. It's one more part of nature and nothing more." Reilly let that statement settle in her mind before continuing. "Now I have to get your temperature down. The water from the spring is cool and I'm going to bathe you in it."

The raging fire that engulfed her was caused by a fever. Leah understood vaguely why she hadn't been able to escape the burning heat. Yet her modesty still wouldn't let her give in to his logic.

"Leave — " She was so weak she could hardly get the words out. "Leave my clothes on."

"I can't. You must have something dry to put on when you come out," Reilly answered. "Don't fight me, Leah. You're going to need your strength."

Her mind resisted, but her body surrendered itself to his expert hands. In a semi-conscious haze she was aware of Reilly bodily lifting her into his arms and carrying her to the water, her head resting against his naked shoulder.

Then she was immersed in water, cooling ripples washing her from head to toe. An arm around her waist kept her from sinking into the refreshing depths of the dammed pool. The overhanging branches of a small willow shaded them from the sun.

Time was in limbo, beyond measurement for Leah.

At some point in her fever-induced stupor, she became aware that Reilly too was unclothed, but it didn't matter as long as the deliciously cool water continued rinsing her fiery skin.

Stirring restlessly, she tried to escape the stifling cocoon that held her tightly. She wanted the refreshing water of the pool to cool her again, A hand gently stroked her temple and settled along her neck. She was lying on the ground in Reilly's arms, the blanket wrapped around them.

"Sleep," he murmured near her ear. "Your fever has broken. You need to sleep."

With shuttered eyes, Leah relaxed against him. The warmth of his body turned into a safe haven instead of a furnace that she needed to escape from. She slept without dreams or nightmares.

Reilly awakened her once in the daylight to feed her some broth. She instantly went back to sleep. Later there was the sensation of him lying beside her.

The next time she opened her eyes, Leah discovered she was alone under the blanket with the sun well up in the sky. The snapping sound of a fire drew her gaze to the center of the miniature glade. Reilly was crouched beside the fire, stirring the contents of the pan sitting near it.

His bronzed torso was shirtless, his muscled chest and shoulders rippling a golden copper in the sunlight. A pair of snug-fitting denim levis covered the lower half of him. As if sensing her gaze, he glanced over his shoulder. The boldly chiselled face was more forcefully handsome than she remembered. Lazily his eyes met her look.

"Hello." The grooves around his mouth deepened with the familiar smile that crinkled his eyes.

"Hello," Leah returned, feeling self-conscious without knowing why.

"Are you hungry?" He poured the liquid from the pan into one of the small bowls.

"A little," she admitted, and tried to shift into a sitting position, only to discover she was weaker than she had realized.

"Lie down. I'll feed you," he said, lithely rising to walk over to her.

"That's squaw's work, isn't it?" An impish smile curved her lips.

The line of his mouth crooked in response. "It is, but an Indian is sometimes forced into the role when his woman is crazy with fever."

Her heart lurched at the term "his woman." He couldn't have meant her to take it literally since he had only been responding in jest to her lighthearted question. Yet it certainly was a heartstopping thought.

Setting the bowl on the ground nearby, Reilly took his backpack, cushioned it with his shirt, and put it beneath her head for a pillow. Cross-legged, he sat beside her and picked up the bowl.

"How many 'moons' have I been out?" Leah asked after swallowing a spoonful of broth put to her lips.

"Three nights." Another spoonful was held to her mouth.

"That long?" she breathed in surprise.

"Try eating without talking," he suggested with amusement, "It will be much faster."

When half the bowl was gone, Leah couldn't manage any more and Reilly set it aside, not forcing her to eat more than she wanted.

"How does your arm feel?" His dark head was tilted to one side, his gaze intently studying her.

Tentatively she moved her left arm, testing it carefully. It was sore, but without that aching throb. She smiled with relief.

"Much better," she nodded.

"You'd better let me have a look at it," he said. "I don't trust your opinion any more." The roguish glint in his eyes removed the sting from his comment.

Without any protest, Leah began unbuttoning her blouse. She was on the third button before she realized she wasn't wearing a bra. Red stained her cheeks a crimson hue as she darted a covert look at Reilly.

"Do you remember that when you were delirious with fever I undressed you to bathe you in the pool?" A black eyebrow arched briefly with question.

Her fingers fumbled with the buttons, neither undoing them nor buttoning them back up. "Yes, I remember." She averted her gaze.

"Your shoulders were chafed from the backpack, so I didn't put your bra back on," he explained.

"I see," she murmured, staring at her fingers clutching the blouse front.

His thumb and forefinger captured her chin and lifted her head to meet the gentle amusement dancing in his eyes. "So did I. Everything there was to see."

Her flush deepened, as did his voice with mockery. "It's pointless to turn prudish now, don't you think?"

Leah's answer was to unbutton her blouse the rest of the way, heat flaming through her veins. While Reilly eased her left arm out of the sleeve, she discreetly shielded her breast with her hand. The blood pounded in her ear.

If he found her action amusing, he made no outward sign. Expertly and impersonally, he examined the wound and rebandaged it, helping her back into the blouse.

"This time I think it will heal," he announced, turning away while she rebuttoned the front. "I could wring your neck for not telling me it was bothering you."

"I thought it was healing," Leah defended self-consciously.

"From now on, let me be the judge." He picked up the bowl and rolled to his feet in one fluid moment, reminding her again of his animal grace. "You'd better get some more rest."

"I've been sleeping for days as it is. I think I should get up before I become permanently bedridden," she stated, fighting the waves of weakness as she tried to sit up.

"There's time enough to try your legs tonight, but you rest this afternoon," Reilly insisted.

She lacked the strength to get up on her own. She had to lie back down. Despite the hours of sleep she had had, she was soon dozing off again.

A purple dusk had settled overhead when she

awoke, casting its violet color on the smooth water of the dammed pool. Chunks of meat sizzled on a spit above a low camp fire. Again Reilly's sixth sense alerted him to Leah's wide-awake state.

"The food is about ready," he stated. "Do you want to sit by the fire?"

"Yes," she answered emphatically.

When he had lifted her to her feet, Leah's long legs felt like quivering sticks of jelly beneath her. She wavered unsteadily toward the fire. She doubted she could have made it even that short distance if it hadn't been for the support of his steady hand at her waist.

Shakily, she sat cross-legged in front of the firs, realizing the full extent of her weakness. Even her hand trembled when she took the bowl of greens Reilly offered her.

"What is this?" she asked.

"I found some rushes growing on the far side of the pool," he answered, spooning the rest into his bowl. "They may be a bit stringy, but they're edible and nourishing."

Actually Leah thought the dish was quite tasty—different and stringy as Reilly had warned, but otherwise good. But it was the tender white quail meat, roasted to perfection on the spit, that really aroused her appetite. She felt positively stuffed as she finished the last piece and licked her fingers in satisfaction.

"That was delicious," she sighed.

"You liked it?" A sideways glance moved briefly over her face.

"Mmmm, did I ever!" Leah pressed a hand against her full stomach. "How did you manage to catch the quail? Did you set a snare?" Unless she had slept very soundly, she hadn't heard any gunshot.

"Quail?" A crooked grin lifted one corner of his mouth.

"That's what it was, wasn't it?" She eyed him curiously.

"No," Reilly drawled the word. "I don't mean to ruin your meal, but it was rattlesnake."

Closing her eyes, Leah quickly swallowed a lump that had suddenly risen in her throat, then took a couple of shaky, calming breaths. Slowly the color returned to her face as the brief nausea passed.

"Is the meal still delicious?" He had been watching her changing expression with wicked laughter in his eyes.

"Maybe not quite as good as it was when I thought I was eating quail," Leah admitted.

Reilly smiled, lighting a cigarette and handing it to her, then lighting one for himself. Their cigarette smoke mingled with the wispy trail from the fire. Although the shock of actually eating snake had worn off, Leah wanted to divert the conversation from food.

"Do you know that in all the time we've been stranded, you've hardly told me anything about yourself? I've rattled on about my parents and Lonnie and my vagabond childhood, but I know very little about you, except that you design turquoise jewelry."

There were a lot of other things she had observed

about him, his calmness in a crisis, his knowledge of the desert, but no actual facts about his life.

"What would you like to know, for instance?" he asked dryly, yet not refusing to divulge personal information about himself.

"I don't know." In truth, Leah wanted to know everything, but she tried to sound lighthearted and nonchalant. "For instance, how did someone who's part Indian get a name like Reilly Smith?"

"You were expecting something more like John Black Feather," Reilly chuckled, exhaling a gauzy cloud of smoke.

"Something like that," she laughed easily at his jesting reply.

"My mother was a half-breed. It's from her that I received my Indian ancestry. The name is from my father, who was Irish." At the questioning arch of Leah's eyebrow, Reilly smiled and nodded. "Yes, although his surname was Smith, he was strictly Irish."

"How?"

"It was common practice years ago for men with questionable pasts to change their names. That's what my father's father did. My father never knew what his real name was, but the family rumor said that my grandfather had killed a man in a bar-room fight back East. No one ever proved whether it was fact or fantasy. One fact is known and that is that he married an Irish lass named Maureen O'Reilly, who was my grandmother. My father left off the 'O' when he named me."

"Are your parents alive?"

"No. My father was killed in a car accident shortly after I was born. And my mother wasn't able to keep me with her, so I was raised by her parents on a reservation. She died when I was eight." Reilly studied the tip of his cigarette for a few silent seconds, then glanced at Leah and smiled almost absently. "Anything else you want to know?"

Leah stared into the fire. Remembering Grady's comment that Reilly was a loner, she was surprised that he had already told her so much about his past. But his last question had invited her to ask more and she definitely wanted to know more.

"What was it like growing up on a reservation?"

"Simple." Knowing that reply was insufficient, he continued, "I went to school with other Indian children, took care of my grandparents' sheep, and helped with other chores. Their home was in an isolated area of semi-desert land. My grandfather made turquoise jewelry as a hobby and a way to supplement their meager income. Whenever I had my work done, he would let me help." A corner of his mouth lifted wryly in memory. "My help was mostly cobbing."

"What's that?" she frowned.

"Separating the turquoise from the host rock with a pair of pliers or a hammer and lead block," Reilly explained. "My grandfather got most of his ore from an abandoned mine in the hills that had been commercially worked out years ago."

"But that's how you got interested in jewelry?"

"Yes." He flicked the cigarette butt into the fire, then looked away to study the first timid stars in the night sky. "In many respects I grew up thinking like an Indian with some of the old customs and traditions, yet I always knew I was mostly white. I never really belonged." When he paused, Leah didn't fill the silence, but waited. "I've never decided whether it was the Indian quarter of my blood desiring freedom that prompted me to leave the reservation or the materialistic white part of me that gave me driving ambition and the desire for a different life."

"You can't divide yourself," Leah murmured. "You're the end product of both worlds, whole and complete."

In her mind, she added more. He was a strong and complete man, creative and intelligent, resourceful and proud. Sewing all those qualities together was a strain of unshakable confidence in himself that gave him an inner peace.

"We're becoming too philosophical," he told her firmly. "I think it's time we went to bed. I'll move it closer to the fire."

While he retrieved the blanket a few feet away, Leah stared at the fire only inches from her knees. "Why do you always make such a small fire? Wouldn't it be warmer if it was larger?"

Reilly spread the blanket beside the fire within arm's reach of the woodpile so the fire could easily be fed during the night.

"The white man makes a large fire, then has to sleep several feet away because it's too hot. The Indian makes a small fire and lies down beside it.'' He held out his hand to help her to her feet, the flickering reflection of the fire dancing in his eyes.

CHAPTER SEVEN

The serenity of the pool was soothing, clear and cool without a ripple to disturb its smoothness. The small water willows curved above it to admire their reflection on its surface. A faint breeze stirred the rushes at the far end while water giggled over the dammed side of the pool to follow the course of the narrow silver stream.

Leaning against a slim tree trunk, Leah plucked at a blade of grass. She was not as weak as she had been yesterday, but her strength was quickly sapped.

A string rested in a curved line on the water, the unravelled threads from one of Reilly's shirts that he had plaited together. The string was attached to one of the lean-to poles and a pin from the first-aid kit was fashioned into a hook on the other end.

A faint, questioning smile touched the edges of her

mouth. "Do you really think there are any fish in the pond?"

"No." Reilly darted her a sideways look, the grooves around his mouth deepened. "But it's an excellent excuse to sit and think."

"Think about what?"

"Things." He shrugged with one shoulder.

"What things?" Leah prompted.

The line of his mouth straightened, leading her to believe that his thoughts were serious ones. He didn't answer immediately.

"This is a good place." His alert gaze swept the area. "There's plenty of water, and firewood too from that deadfall over there."

"And it's peacefully beautiful," Leah added to his practical assessment. "We were lucky to find it."

"Against the earth tones of the desert, a patch of green stands out for miles. And where there's green, there's water," he replied. "I noticed it when we were almost at the bottom of the mountain."

Turning her gaze to the mountains that ringed them on three sides, Leah tried to locate the saddle-backed ridge on which their plane had crashed. Each mountain and ridge bore a likeness to another and she couldn't find it.

"Where were we?" she asked.

"About thirty miles back and up." Reilly pointed toward a mountain peak that didn't seem very far away. "Do you see the small dip on the other side of that peak? That's where the plane crashed."

Sighing, she leaned back against the tree. "I

imagine we've been given up for dead after all this time."

This was the eighth day. It seemed like such a short amount of time, yet conversely, it seemed like forever. "It will be another three or four days before you'll have the strength to try to walk out of here," he stated grimly.

"At least here we won't have to worry about a supply of water," Leah offered. "And let's hope we'll have food."

This morning Reilly had announced that the three remaining packets of dried food would be used only as a last resort. They would eat what they were able to forage. He had placed snares along the game trails leading to the watering hole. If that failed, he would hunt with his pistol and there was always the abundant supply of snakes to fall back on. Although Leah doubted she would be able to eat them with the same degree of pleasure as she had when she hadn't known beforehand.

"With the two of us, the food we have now would last only three days. It would last six days, if there was only one," he said quietly, slowly trailing the string through the water.

Something in his tone made her stiffen. "What's that supposed to mean?"

His impassive face turned to meet her challenging look. "That you stay here while I go for help."

"We've been over that before," she stated tautly.

"Circumstances are different. You aren't capable of traveling, not for several days." Reilly averted his attention back to the fishing line. "I noticed a dirt track about ten miles from here. It heads down the center of the valley floor. It will either lead to the highway or a ranch house."

"How far?"

"I don't know. I haven't seen any smoke to the south in the morning that might indicate the existence of a ranch house," he answered thoughtfully. "The second day we were here I walked over to the track. There wasn't any sign that it had been used for several weeks or longer. It might have been abandoned when the mine was. But it leads somewhere."

"I won't stay here alone, Reilly. I mean it." Her teeth were clenching in determination.

"The longer we stay out here, the more risk we'll be taking that something will happen. You'll be safe here by yourself."

"You said we were in this together," Leah reminded him. "I won't let you leave without me."

"You're too weak to go now."

"I am not!" she protested vigorously even though she knew what Reilly said was true. "I can walk just as far and just as long as you can! There's nothing wrong with me. My fever's gone and I'm as healthy as a horse!"

To prove her allegation, she rose swiftly to her feet and took a quick step toward him, but sudden movement instantly made her dizzy. She pressed a hand to her reeling head and swayed unsteadily.

With split second reaction, Reilly was on his feet, hands gripping her waist in support. She leaned heavily against him, fighting to regain her sense of balance. He lifted her in his arms and set her back against the slim trunk.

"Now will you admit I'm right?" His green eyes mocked the pallor of her face. "You are too weak."

"I moved too quickly, that's all," Leah defended, resting her head against the tree to gaze at the man kneeling beside her. "I swear that you're not leaving without me, Reilly. If you go, I'll follow." There was a tight lump in her throat as she spoke, but her voice was otherwise controlled.

Grim amusement was carved in his features. "I believe you mean that." Pivoting on his knee, he started to move away.

But Leah needed assurance that he had changed his mind and wouldn't leave her. She clutched at the material of his shirt to halt his departure.

"Reilly?" She leaned forward, earnestly searching his expression with questing hazel eyes.

Motionless, he held her look, revealing nothing of his thoughts or decision. A smoldering light of anger burned in his eyes and his hand slid slowly, almost unwillingly, along the back of her waist.

Her heart fluttered uncertainly, excited and afraid. Then his mouth was savagely crushing hers in a punishing kiss. The pain lasted only brief seconds as Reilly switched the kiss to sensual demand. Response flamed through Leah's veins, melting her against the solid wall of his chest.

The weight of his body pressed her backward, pinning her on the carpet of grass while he continued to explore her mouth with a rousing thoroughness. Shudders of primitive rapture quivered within her. She had not guessed that his masterful kiss would be as glorious as this. Her senses were reeling under the assault of his desire.

The soft flesh of her body molded itself willingly to the male length of him. No part of her was immune to his fire. His caressing fingers explored her neck and shoulders, blazing a trail that his mouth followed. Quicksilver gasps of air were all she was allowed before a new shiver of experience stole her breath.

In a mindless haze, she knew she had lost control and was powerless to regain it as long as his lips kept returning to dominate hers. Unexpectedly, Reilly rolled on to his back, drawing her on top of him. There he cupped her face in his hands and held it away from him.

Her parted lips were swollen and trembling from his kisses. She knew her eyes had darkened from the desire he had aroused. Her lashes fell to veil the completeness of her response. Yet she couldn't deny the truth of what she felt.

"I've wanted you to do that." Her voice throbbed with the disturbed beat of her heart.

"Leah." His husky tone betrayed his inner passion too, yet his was controlled. "You've never known a man, have you?"

The gently spoken question frightened her as his embrace had not. The silken curtain of her hair had fallen forward. It shielded the flames that licked her cheeks as she drew away from his unresisting hands

and scrambled shakily to her feet. She could feel his
piercingly alert eyes watching her, but she was unable
to meet them. Keeping her back to him, she stuffed her
trembling hands deep in the pockets of her slacks and
drew a quivering breath. "Have you?" repeated
Reilly.

The question came from directly behind her, his
animal silence bringing him to his feet unheard by
her. In the next instant, his hands were resting lightly
on each side of her waist. She breathed in sharply to
keep from turning and seeking his embrace.

"I . . . I really don't see why I should answer that,"
she swallowed, closing her eyes and wishing she could
close the rest of her senses to his nearness.

"I want to know," he replied simply.

"You could have found it out for yourself. I could
scream my head off and there's no one for miles to
hear me. What stopped you?" Leah challenged, but
with a faintly hysterical note.

"Dammit, Leah!" He spun her around, exasperation snapping in his green eyes.

The pinched lines around her nose and mouth must
have betrayed her inexperienced state because Reilly
immediately loosened his steel grip on her waist, the
fire in his gaze banking at the sight of the apprehension that clouded her eyes.

Reilly smiled gently. "You don't need to be
afraid."

"Of who?" she blinked. His touch was curling her
toes. "Of you? Or me?"

His muscular chest rose in a deep breath, his eyes

narrowing into green slits. "You shouldn't say such things."

"Why?" Leah challenged. "I can't deny that a moment ago I wanted you to make love to me!"

"Well, try!" he snapped savagely, releasing her from his hold.

The anger that had flashed across his face for that split second was completely gone when Leah focused her gaze on him. The mask of unshakable composure covered his lean features.

Leah felt trapped in a labyrinth with no escape in sight. She was thoroughly confused and puzzled by his actions. Reilly had wanted her—she wasn't so inexperienced that she didn't know that. Yet when he had discovered she was a virgin, he had rejected her. Why? Because she wasn't sufficiently experienced for his tastes?

Hot tears filled her eyes. "I don't understand you, Reilly Smith!" she lashed out at him angrily.

A furrow of absent concentration darkened his brow as he glanced briefly in her direction. "It's simple," he replied harshly. "When I'm in the desert, I think too much like an Indian."

The cryptic answer made more sense than his actions. Leah rubbed the back of her neck in frustration and tried to check the welling tears. She held them back, but she couldn't keep her chin from trembling.

A sigh came from Reilly. Grass whispered beneath his feet as he rose and walked to her. His hands touched her shoulders and Leah drew away. He simply grasped them more firmly a second time.

"Please don't try to convince me that you're some saint," she declared caustically, tossing back her head to glare at him defiantly through her mist of tears.

"I'm not virtuous by any means," Reilly agreed with iron control, "although I don't intend to brag about the number of women I've known."

"That's a relief!" Her tongue tasted bitter with sarcasm.

"If a maiden is taken by a man before marriage, in the eyes of the Indian, she becomes unclean and is shunned." The faint cynicism in his tone seemed to be directed at himself. "That's a quaint custom to be observed in these promiscuous times, I'll admit. Nevertheless," he drew the words out slowly, "as far as you are concerned, I'm compelled to respect my grandfather's teachings. We have been through too much together these past days for me to be the one to take away your innocence."

A tremulous smile touched her mouth. His words chased the clouds away from her heart and let the radiant light of joy shine through.

"That's why you asked," she breathed.

"Yes." Reilly smiled without humor.

Slipping her arms around his middle, she sighed contentedly, nestling her head against his chest. His arms tightened to hold her close, a firm hand slowly caressing her shoulders and back as his mouth roughly moved against her hair. His fingers raked through her hair, drawing her head back. His mouth closed over hers in a hard lingering kiss. The melting of her bones began all over again.

When he released her, his eyes burned possesively over her face. "I think it's time you took charge of the fishing while I check the snares," Reilly said huskily.

"Let me go with you," Leah whispered.

His fingers covered her mouth as he shook his dark head. "I want to be sure you've had plenty of rest so you'll be able to cook dinner tonight." He pushed her to the ground near where his pole lay.

Leah didn't resist and sat quietly on the bank while he walked away. She knew she was falling in love with him, if she hadn't already. Was it because she couldn't have survived in this desert wilderness without him? She thought not. She admired his competency, resourcefulness and strength, but her feelings for him went beyond that. Nor was what she felt strictly physical.

So, eliminating all the other possibilities, she was in love with him. She tried to caution her heart that eight days was a very short time to fall in love with someone. Her heart answered that she and Reilly had been through more than some couples experience in a lifetime together.

The only uncertainty that remained was how Reilly felt about her. If for him, it was more than physical attraction, too? Leah sighed, knowing that no one would ever put words in his mouth nor elicit an answer he wasn't prepared to make. But, for the moment, the knowledge of her love for him was enough.

One of the snares had trapped a rabbit. Reilly had cleaned it and shown Leah how to roast it on the spit. Again, their menu had contained a side dish of greens, an item that Leah had decided was going to become a staple part of their diet.

The exertion from doing their few dishes left her slightly weak. She set them near the fire to dry. Brushing a hand wearily through her gold-brown hair, she wished longingly for a hot bath and a shampoo.

"Tired?" Reilly asked gently.

"A little," Leah admitted. She sat down beside him in front of the fire, curling her legs beneath her. "Mostly I was thinking that I was a mess."

An arm circled her waist and drew her against his shoulder, locking his hands across her stomach as he kept her faced towards the fire. Leah stared into the flames, a feeling of intense bliss stealing over her.

"Aren't you going to say that I'm not a mess?" she teased with a soft sigh of contentment.

"I'm not going to state the obvious," Reilly chuckled.

"Now that's a tactful reply!" Her head moved briefly in mock exasperation, but there was amusement in her tone.

A coyote sang his lament to the winking eye of a crescent moon. On a faraway hill, another coyote joined in the chorus. Overhead, the stars blazed brightly in the velvet sky.

His chin brushed the top of her hair. "Did you want me to say that your hair is perfumed with sage and smoke? That its color reminds me of the dappled coat of a doe fawn in the morning sunlight?'' The husky murmur of his voice quickened her heartbeat.

"Is that really what you think?" Leah held her breath.

Reilly smiled against her hair. "Your eyes are the color of the fawn's, round and trusting, fringed with sunbrowned lashes.'' A hand circled her wrist to make her arm join his as he drew her more tightly into the circle of his arms. "Your bones are deceivingly dainty as a fawn's.''

"I think''—she was sinking in a quicksand of heady emotions, yet not wanting to struggle to the point where she could break free "that one of your ancestors kissed the Blarney Stone, Reilly Smith.''

"Do you?" he mused softly against her hair. 'It comes naturally from both sides of my heritage. Some of the greatest orators in our history were Indians—Red Cloud, Spotted Tail—if only someone had listened.''

There was no bitterness in his statement and nothing that required a response. The desert silence moved in, drawing them into its magic circle of ageless enchantment.

It was a long time before either of them moved until Reilly finally decreed softly that it was time they got some sleep. The only thing that made Leah willingly agree was the knowledge that she would return to his arms beneath the blanket

This night, as he cradled her in his arms, she lifted her head for a kiss. The firm pressure of his mouth on hers started a slow glow of warmth through her limbs. The small fire remained even after he had dragged his mouth from hers, leaving it tingling and moist from his kiss. The steady beat of his heart beneath her head soon lulled her to sleep.

Cool air invaded the blanket cocoon. Leah frowned at its chill, keeping her eyes tightly shut, and tried to snuggle closer against Reilly's muscular length. He wasn't there!

She was immediately awake. Soft morning light filled the camp. The flames of the campfire were hungrily devouring the fresh wood that had been added. Throwing back the cover, she sat up. There was no sign of Reilly.

The canteen was gone. Her gaze flew to the waterhole several yards away, thinking Reilly was there refilling the canteen with water. He wasn't. Scrambling to her feet, Leah scanned the area around the campfire again.

A cold dread filled her heart. "He couldn't. He wouldn't!" she murmured aloud, protesting against the chilling thought.

But it was entirely possible. Reilly was nowhere to be seen. That left only the desert. Shuddering, Leah realized that he had not promised he wouldn't leave without her. In fact, he had never said that he wouldn't go.

Her gaze shifted toward the center of the valley. He had sneaked away at first light, probably thinking she would be too frightened and weak to follow.

Leah clenched her teeth tightly together. "You're in for a surprise, Reilly Smith!" she muttered.

Deciding that he couldn't be very far ahead of her, she kicked sand on to the fire, quickly stirred the smoldering embers, and kicked on more sand. If she hurried, she could catch up to him.

There was no point trying to carry the few items with her. Their weight would slow her down. Reilly had the canteen and that was the important thing.

Not allowing time to question the wisdom of her impulse, Leah abandoned the campsite without a backward glance. Her only thought was to catch up with Reilly as quickly as possible. She started running, wanting to make up the distance that separated them.

The desert brush whipped at her legs and thighs. A startled flock of mountain bluebirds skimmed the bush tops in flight. All her attention was focused on the land ahead of her.

Leah's scream ripped the air as an unknown force yanked her backward. Her motion stopped with an impact against a a hard, immovable object.

"Where the hell do you think you were going?" Reilly demanded shaking her savagely by the shoulders.

She stared at his glaring, angry face in disbelief.

"Reilly!" She started laughing and crying at the same time, ceasing her instinctive struggle of self-protection.

"Answer me!" His eyes glittered coldly.

"I thought—" her breath came in short, laughingly

relieved signs, "I thought you'd gone for help. I thought you'd left me."

"You crazy—" Reilly snapped off the rest of the words, leaving it dangling, unfinished in the air. "And you were coming after me."

Leah bobbed her head, trying to calm her shaky breath. "I told you I would," she reminded him.

His fingers loosened their digging grip into her bones. "You might have checked to be certain I was gone," he replied tightly, "instead of racing off into the bush like a madwoman."

"I looked for you," she defended. "Where were you?"

"Checking the snares." He released her entirely, standing in front of her, his hands on his hips, his expression grim and unyielding.

Her hazel eyes rolled guiltily away from his censorious gaze. She had completely forgotten about the snares in her panicked certainty that he had left her.

"I didn't remember them," she admitted.

Reilly breathed in deeply, his action letting her know what he thought of that. "Let's go back to camp and restart the fire." His mouth thinned sardonically. "You were so intent on following me, would you like to follow me back to camp?"

Leah nodded. There was no doubt he was angry with her. In retrospect, her action was foolhardy and impulsive. She could very easily have got lost.

"How—" She had to hurry to keep up with his long strides. "How did you know where I'd gone?"

"I didn't," he replied curtly, "but I heard the racket of something charging through the bush, and I decided it was either you or a stampeding herd of cattle."

"I was stupid," sighed Leah.

He slid her a chilling look. "If you expect me to disagree, woman, you're wrong."

Until his anger cooled, Leah decided it was better to keep silent. It became an oppressive silence, as she patiently rebuilt the fire. When it was burning freely once more, he began cleaning a gamebird he had caught in the snare. Not a word nor a glance did he direct at Leah.

There was little for her to do except sit and watch him, squirming inwardly at the uncomfortable silence. The feeling kept growing that she was being unfairly punished. Finally she decided that it was time for a truce to be offered.

As Reilly started to put the cleaned bird on the spit, Leah stepped forward. "Let me do that. It's squaw's work." She tried to lessen the crackling tension by drawing on their stand-by joke.

"You aren't a squaw." The aloof indifference in his voice cut like a knife.

"Reilly, I'm sorry. What more do you want me to say?" she demanded.

With the bird secured on the spit, he stood up, his chiselled features carved into uncompromisingly harsh lines. "Do you realize you could have got yourself killed out there? If not from snakebite or a broken neck, then from thirst or starvation! You didn't take anything to protect you from the elements! You didn't take any food or water!''

"I wanted to catch up with you!" Leah shouted in answer to his loud accusing voice. "I didn't want to be slowed down carrying things. Besides, you had the canteen! Was I supposed to go racing through the desert carrying a pan of water?''

"You shouldn't have been racing anywhere! And if I had left, then you should have stayed here! And I took the canteen to refill it at the waterhole on my way to check the snares!''

"But I didn't know that!" she protested angrily.

His eyes narrowed as he let out a long, exasperated breath. "I ought to take you over my knee and spank the living tar out of you for what you put me through," he declared through gritted teeth.

"What about what I went through?" Leah retorted. "I thought you'd gone off and left me!''

"So you followed, not knowing where you were going and not taking anything with you. You would have been lost—or dead before the day was out," Reilly said harshly.

"At least then you would have been rid of me and you wouldn't have been thinking about me any more! Aren't you sorry you went after me and brought me back!" she cried bitterly, brushing her hair away from her face as she turned away.

She was spun back around and pulled against his chest in one fluid motion. Her startled mouth opened to protest and it was covered with his brutal kiss. Love rushed, unchecked, to respond to the punishing ardor of his mouth. Her senses whirled in the vortex of Reilly's embrace until she didn't know down from up and didn't care.

Then his mouth was buried in the sensitive cord along her neck. "You would test the patience and endurance of a saint," he muttered against her skin.

His warm breath was a disturbing caress as she wound her arms tightly around his middle for support. The wild tempo of her heart was making clear thinking difficult. She inhaled deeply of his intoxicating male scent and sighed.

"You're not a saint," she murmured.

His hands firmly set her away from him. The dark fire glittering in his eyes did nothing to steady the erratic beat of her heart. His mouth crooked wryly.

"Don't remind me." There was no more cold anger in his expression. "See what you can do about keeping our breakfast and lunch from being burned up while I wash."

The fire was trying to char one side of the dressed fowl. Leah was forced to rescue it as Reilly walked toward the narrow stream formed by the water spilling over the dam's walls. As she turned the spit, she watched him crouch beside the stream, splashing the cold water on his face and the back of his neck.

Smiling at his action, she glanced at the sun. Its fiery heat hadn't yet begun to scorch the ground. In fact, it was only pleasantly warm.

CHAPTER EIGHT

After they had eaten, Reilly had suggested that Leah
rest in the shade through the hot hours of early
afternoon. She tried, knowing that it was important to
regain her strength, but she couldn't relax.

A fever burned inside as she watched him repairing
one of the snares. It wasn't a fever caused by infection,
unless love was infectious. If it was, she hoped Reilly
caught the disease, too.

No matter how often she closed her eyes, they
opened, her gaze strayed to Reilly. Her senses would
tingle with the awareness of him. The ache to be in his
arms would start again and all thought of rest
immediately vanished.

It wasn't any use. She stopped trying to force
inactivity upon herself. She recognized the inherent
temptation of their present situation, the two of them

alone in a miniature paradise, the succulent apple waiting for the bite that would lead her into true womanhood.

Pushing herself up from the cool carpet of grass, Leah briskly rubbed her hands over her hipbones. Reilly's questioning look flickered curiously over her determined expression.

"I'm going to wash my clothes down at the stream," she announced. "If you want, I'll do your shirt." She tried to sound offhand and partially succeeded. "I'm not in the mood to lie around doing nothing," she explained in unnecessary defence of her decision.

His shirt was already unbuttoned and hanging loose in front. With a nod of acceptance to her offer, he slipped it off and tossed it to her, immediately returning his attention to the damaged snare.

"You can wear one of the shirts we used for a backpack while you're washing your clothes." His dark head remained bent over his task.

"Thanks." Only he seemed not to hear her reply.

Behind the screen of a thick bush, Leah stripped away her outer clothes and donned the robe-like shirt, its tails reaching halfway down her thighs to provide relatively decent coverage over her underwear. Rolling back the sleeves, she set to work rinsing and rubbing to try to clean their clothes minus the assistance of detergent.

Finally she decided they were as clean as she was going to get them under the circumstances. With the back of her hand, she wiped the beads of perspiration from her forehead and lip, then picked up the wet clothes and carried them to the large stands of sunburnt brush on the edge of their spring-made glade.

The sun will fry them in minutes, she smiled to herself, feeling the scorching rays of the sun the instant she stepped out of the shade. More prespiration collected between her shoulder blades as she laid the clothes over the bushes. She glanced longingly at the dammed pool of water, about three times the size of a bathtub.

She retreated into the shade. "Reilly? Would it hurt anything if I got my arm wet?"

"Why? Did you get it wet?" He frowned, but didn't glance up.

"No," Leah denied quickly. "If it wouldn't hurt anything I was going to take a short dip in the waterhole to cool off."

"You'd better let me take a look at it first." As he lifted his head, his gaze slid over her in absent appraisal.

"Just a minute." She turned her back to him and slipped her left arm out of the rolled shirt sleeve, wrapping the left side of her shirt in sarong fashion across her front.

There was a flicker of amusement in his green eyes at her action as he rose to his feet to examine the wound. His touch against her skin was strictly impersonal when he eased the bandage away.

"You're going to have a scar from this, do you

know that?'' he commented, adjusting the bandage back in place.

"It doesn't matter," Leah shrugged. It was difficult to breathe naturally with Reilly standing so close. The nakedness of his bronzed chest ignited all sorts of wayward desires. She tried to shut them out as she tossed her head to look at his face. "Will it hurt if I get it wet?"

His gaze fastened itself on her mouth. For a heartstopping moment Leah felt herself start to sway toward him, aching with every fiber of her being to feel his caress. The silver and turquoise necklace gleamed dully against the tanned column of his neck.

Briskly he turned away. "I don't think so, but if I were you, I'd try to keep it out of the water. There's no need to take a risk at this stage. The waterhole isn't deep. Unless you slip, you shouldn't have any trouble keeping the bandage dry."

"How do you know it isn't deep?" Leah arched a curious cycbrow, frowning slightly.

"I bathed you in it once to bring your fever down, remember?" Reilly reminded her with lazy mockery in his tone as he again bent over the snare. "And I've used it myself a few times—in the mornings before you were awake."

No wonder he always looked so fresh and impervious to the rigors of their less than luxurious conditions, she thought. But there was hardly a need to make a vocal comment on the fact.

"I'll be careful not to slip," she promised diffidently.

At the waterhole, Leah glanced over her shoulder
Reilly's back was turned toward her, deliberately or
indifferently, she didn't know which.

Removing the shirt the rest of the way, she stepped
into the pool, using an overhanging branch of
willow for balance. The deepest point, near the far end
of the pool, brought the water to her waist. The
temperature of the water in that area was several
degrees cooler than the rest of the pool. She decided
that she was near the spring's inlet.

It was awkward keeping her left arm out of the
water while she tried to rinse the upper half of her
body and her hair. It was a slow procedure but
refreshingly cooling. She resisted the impulse to
linger, splashing and playing in the water, and
crawled on to the bank. Reilly was still working on the
snare.

Quickly she towelled the moisture from her skin
with the shirt she had been wearing, blotting the
excess water from her undergarments. The rest of her
clothes would be dry. Slipping the now damp shirt on
Leah retraced her path to the bushes, collected the
washed clothes, and changed swiftly into her own.

The seams of her slacks were still damp, but that
coolness and her damp underwear countered the
sunbaked heat of the dry material of her slacks and
blouse.

"Here's your shirt," she told Reilly as she returned
to the circle of their camp.

"Hang it on the lean-to." His jet dark head nodded

toward it while his attention remained with the damaged snare.

Leah hooked the collar over one of the poles. "Haven't you fixed that yet? You've been working on it all afternoon."

"Whatever it was that was caught in it worked on it all night," he replied absently.

Kneeling beside the stack of their meager possessions, she sifted impatiently through them, finally sitting on her heels and glancing at Reilly.

"Do you know where the comb is?" she asked.

"In the food box."

She found it and began raking its teeth through her tousled and snarled hair. The sun had bleached pale streaks through its light brown color, increasing the golden highlights. As she tugged the comb through her hair, she watched a cloud shadow racing across a distant mountain slope. A ghost moon occupied a corner of the daylight sky.

There had not been a sign of a search plane in the last two days. There couldn't have been one previously or Reilly would have mentioned it. There was no one who knew where they were or that they were alive.

Leah thought of her father, stern yet compassionate, but always correct and proper. His air of reserve was a contrast to her mother's warm, outgoing personality, which helped her make new friends with ease every time her husband was transferred.

With his cold logic, her father would have calculated Leah's chances of surviving the plane crash and nine days in a desert wilderness. She guessed that his conclusion would be that there was little hope that she was still alive. He would be devoting himself to consoling her mother. Lonnie, she knew, would never give up the search until he found her. He did not accept the inevitable as their father did.

Her father's calculations could not have taken into consideration Reilly's presence. He couldn't know of Reilly's knowledge of the desert or his ability to live with relatively little hardship in primitive conditions.

A smile played with her mouth as she visualized her parents' reaction if they were able to witness this scene—Reilly sitting there trying to repair a broken snare to catch their night's meal and herself combing her hair after washing their clothes in a stream and bathing in a pool.

The clock could have been turned back a hundred years. The only modern possessions they had with them were a flashlight, an emergency ration of food, a pistol, and a pocket-knife. Everything else they had made or improvised—the pan, the bowls, the spoons. the snares, the lean-to.

"Why are you smiling?" Reilly was studying her, his impassive face tipped to one side in idle curiosity.

"I was imagining my parents' astonishment if they could see us now, living here in the desert like natives." Her smile deepened with wryness.

He nodded understandingly, his gaze briefly sweeping the sky before returning to the snare in his lap. His action wiped the smile from her face.

"There isn't much hope any more that a plane will

find us, is there?'' Leah said. "We'll have to walk out of here, won't we?''

"Yes.'' A simple, clear-cut answer.

Her gaze shifted to the sage-colored valley and the corridor of mountain that enclosed it. The valley seemed to run for ever. It was difficult to remember that somewhere beyond the horizon, there was a modern highway with cars and trucks and buildings and homes with electricity, running water, and central heat and air-conditioning. The neon world of Las Vegas was an absolute fantasy in the cruel beauty of this wilderness.

A snarl at the back of her head caught the comb's teeth. She tried working the comb through the knotted hair and she gasped at the inadvertent yank on her scalp. The sound drew a look from Reilly.

"A rat built a nest in my hair,'' she answered the silent question in the green eyes.

While she tried to work out the snarl, she watched him set up the snare to test his repairs. At the first pressure, it snapped at the very place he had mended. Reilly gathered it up and tossed it in the banked fire.

"Can't you fix it?'' Leah protested as a tiny flame licked greedily over the snare.

He shook his head in a negative answer. "The other three will have to be enough.'' His sideways glance noted her struggles with the comb. "Want some help?''

"Please,'' she sighed with frustration. "I can't see what I'm doing,'' she rubbed the tender portion of her scalp that had become sore from repeated pulling of her knotted hair, "although I certainly can feel it!"

Rising, he walked to her, taking the comb from her hand as he knelt behind her. With gentle care, he worked the hair free of its snarling knot piece by piece, then smoothed the hair into the rest curling around her shoulders. He offered the comb to Leah.

"Would you comb the rest of it . . . to be sure there aren't any more knots?" It was only an excuse to keep him near. The breathless tremor in her voice must have betrayed her inner wish.

"Leah, no." His answer was grimly firm.

He tossed the comb on the ground in front of her. She turned sideways, her hazel eyes wide and shimmering with the aching need of her love for the sustenance of his touch. The parted softness of her lips issued an invitation that his jade eyes couldn't ignore.

His narrowed gaze ripped away from her mouth to look deep into her eyes. "You're playing a dangerous game, Leah," he muttered.

"I know," she swallowed tightly, her voice unreasonably calm, "but—"

"This situation provides enough temptations without you offering more," he added flatly.

Leah averted her gaze, lowering her chin in reluctant agreement. "You're right, of course," she admitted, but it didn't soothe her wildly leaping pulse.

A sun-browned hand lightly cupped her cheek and chin, turning it back to meet his gaze. Desire smoldered through the sooty veil of his lashes as it swept possessively over her upturned face.

"I should have left this morning and gone for help."

She moved her cheek against his fingers, her lashes fluttering briefly from the magic spell of his touch. "I would have followed you."

"I know." Her lips curved into a faint smile.

An irresistible force bent his dark head toward her. At the touch of his mouth against hers, Leah turned into his arms, sliding her hands around his neck into the black thickness of his hair.

The demand of his kiss tilted her head backward while his molding hands arched her against him. A fire to equal the burning rays of the sun flamed through her veins, the roar of its blaze raging in her ears. The male scent of him was intoxicating fuel to the fire that consumed her.

Boneless, she gasped as his mouth explored the exposed hollow of her throat, sending volcanic shudders through her body from his sensually arousing caress. Pushing aside the collar of her blouse, his mouth tantalized her shoulder, trailing up the sensitive cord of her neck to nibble at her ear lobe. Then he teased the corner of her mouth until her lips sought his kiss.

The iron band of his arms eased her to the ground. Leah's hands slipped to his muscular shoulders to draw him with her, then remained to revel in the nakedness of his hard flesh. Crushed beneath his weight and smothered by his kiss, she could hardly breathe, yet there was no thought to struggle. Never before had she been so completely alive.

The sun blazed white-hot in the sky. Behind her closed eyes, the light of love was as intensely bright as the sun, searing in its insatiable fire and illuminating every corner of her heart. It was beyond physical. If Reilly never touched her again, Leah knew the invisible linkage of love bound her to him for eternity.

Wordlessly, she responded to his embrace with all the fervor the magic knowledge had given her. The soaring joy that sang in her veins lifted her to a horizonless world. Reilly's kiss hardened as if he had been carried there, too.

Then just as suddenly, as if the height was too dizzying, he rolled on his side, his hand slipping away from her breast to rub his face and mouth. One arm couldn't let her go. It remained to hold her firmly against his chest.

Dazed by the rapturous discovery, Leah could only listen to the pagan drumbeat of his heart and the raggedness of his breathing. Much slower, she descended from the spiritual plateau to the physical reality of their nearly consummated embrace. Irrationally she knew she would have gloried in his possession of her and cared not about any future consequences.

His control was almost frightening when she considered how readily she had abandoned her own under the possession of her love. The wonder of it kept her silent for several minutes.

"Reilly." Her voice was warm and throbbing.

His hand cupped her cheek, a thumb touching her mouth to ask for silence. "Leah"—she could hear the conflict with his physical need in his husky voice—"be still."

It would have been easy to disobey his order and persuade him to countermand it. The delicious temptation teased her thoughts, but the wisdom behind it was unquestionable. So she lay unmoving in the half-embrace of his arm until she felt the tension easing from his muscles and knew he was again in total command.

"Tell me about your boyfriend," he said quietly.

Her eyebrows drew together in confusion, "Who?" Leah blinked.

"Marvin, the man you've been dating."

Tipping back her head, she gazed into Reilly's impassive features. "How did you know about him?" she frowned.

"You mentioned him when you were delirious." He smiled, but it didn't reach his eyes.

It was strange, but she couldn't remember what Marvin looked like. It seemed years ago since she had seen him. The vague image she could summon was of a pale, insignificant man compared to Reilly, lacking the masculine vitality and virility that were a dominant part of the man who now held her in his arms.

"He works at the same bank as I do," she answered indifferently. "I've been out with him several times, which, I suppose, classified him as a boyfriend. What did I say about him?"

"Nothing."

She believed him. There was little she could have

said about Marv except that he was nice and possessive in an irritating kind of way. A stab of jealousy shifted her thoughts to an adjoining track.

"Tell me about your girlfriend," she requested tensely.

"I don't think that terminology would fit." His mouth twisted cynically as he shifted on to his back and stared at the pale blue sky.

An agonizing pain knotted her insides. "Your mistress, then," she suggested with underlying bitterness. "Tell me about her. Does she . . . live with you?"

His dark head shifted to the side to look down at her nestled in the crook of his arm, his hair pitch black against the green of the long grass.

"I live by myself," he answered, a remoteness in his tone. "My mistress is my work. I know women, but I don't have a woman."

His reply should have made her feel content. Instead she felt a vague dissatisfaction. It was several seconds before she realized why. The implication of his answer included her in the category of women in the plural. A lump rose in her throat.

"You . . . you mentioned you lived in Las Vegas," she murmured, needing to change the subject. "Where?"

"I have a house in the foothills outside the city."

"Why . . . er . . . why did you pick Las Vegas?" Leah tried to sound nonchalant.

"It's centrally located for my work. I'm not far from

the mines or the outlets for my work in California and Arizona.''

"Do you spend much time at your home?''

"A good deal, yes.''

Again, Leah tilted back her head to see his face, smiling bravely despite the tears scalding the back of her eyes. "When we get back, shall I see you?''

The pause before he answered was electric. The jade mask of his gaze revealed nothing to her searching eyes. "I imagine we'll have dinner one evening,'' Reilly seemed to choose his words carefully, "to celebrate our safe return.''

It was better than nothing. Averting her gaze, she slid her hand over the naked flatness of his stomach. "I'd like that,'' she agreed with aching softness.

Her wrist was seized and her hand jerked away from the firmness of his flesh. The motion continued, turning her on to her back, her arms pinned above her head as Reilly hovered above her, dark anger flashing in his eyes.

"Don't do that!'' he snapped harshly. "Do you think I'm made of stone?''

"I'm sorry.'' She knew she should be frightened by the suppressed violence in his expression, but she wasn't. "I can't help it, Reilly, I—''

"Yes, you can!'' Abruptly he released her wrists and got to his feet. His expression was cold and grim as he towered above her. "You know as well as I do what's happening between us!'' He turned away, savagely rubbing the back of his neck. "We've been alone out here too long. The world we lived in before the crash seems far removed from today. But we're going to get back," he added firmly. "When we do, these days we've spent together will be the time that seems unreal."

"Is that what you think?" There was a calm curiousness to Leah's voice. Having concrete instead of desert sand beneath her feet would not alter the love she felt for him.

"It's the way life is." It was a statement not issued to be debated. With a long stride, Reilly grabbed his shirt from the lean-to pole. "I'm going to check the snares."

Was he telling her something? Leah wondered as she watched him go. Was he saying not to fall in love with him because he was not in love with her? She picked up the comb from where he had tossed it and began running it through her hair, digging the teeth into her scalp to stop the chilling numbness from totally possessing her.

By early evening, Reilly hadn't left her to walk for help. He was too wise in the ways of the desert to get lost checking the snares he had set some distance from the waterhole.

As dusk settled over the sky, Leah clutched the flashlight tightly in her hand. If he wasn't back by the time the sun touched the rim of the mountain, she was going out to look for him. She added another log to the fire and glanced at the mountain.

There wasn't a whisper of a sound, yet something made her spin around. Where there had been nothing but cobweb shadows cast by the willows Reilly stood, returning to the camp with the animal silence of his ancestors.

Only when she saw him did Leah realize how numbly she had waited for him to come back. Relief weakened her knees, keeping her from racing into his arms. Relief, and the withdrawn expression in his face. His gaze studied her slowly, sliding finally to the flashlight in her hand.

"I   I was coming to look for you," she explained shakily. "I thought if you weren't back by sundown, that you had got hurt somehow."

His expression didn't alter as he slipped the pistol from his waistband and returned it to the first-aid kit. Then his swinging strides carried him to the fire.

"Where did you go?" Leah asked when he offered no explanation for his long absence.

Except for the perspiration stains on his shirt, there wasn't a mark on his leanly muscled physique. His impassivity chilled her to the bone.

"The snares were empty." He took a long drink from the canteen, avoiding her searching eyes. "I went hunting—unsuccessfully."

Leah hugged her arms about her to ward off the sudden attack of misery. "I'm not hungry." She stared into the fire.

"You're going to eat anyway," he stated firmly.

A sighing, bitter laugh escaped her throat. "Yes, I have to get my strength back, don't I?"

"Yes, you do." His gaze narrowed on her huddled form for a slashing second.

Leah looked at his carved profile, so aggressively

male. His black hair had grown longer since the crash and now curled over the short collar. The shirt was opened in the front, revealing the hard bronzed chest. Muscles rippled as he recapped the canteen. The ache to touch him was a physical pain.

"Reilly—" Her voice throbbed with need.

Was it her imagination or had his face grown paler beneath his tan? A muscle twitched alongside his lean jaw, but he didn't glance at her.

"I'll refill the canteen while you decide which one of the packages you want to fix tonight." He turned away from the fire.

His movement brought Leah to her feet. "I'm not hungry now.

"Reilly, will you listen to me?" she demanded in frustration. He crouched along the pool's bank, letting the canteen float on the water. "Reilly, I'm in love with you." She thought she would have burst if she had held the admission back much longer.

Her statement brought no reaction. He didn't even blink an eye at her words. He just watched the water flowing into the canteen. Somehow Leah had to make him understand that she meant it.

"I know you think this physical attraction we feel is a—a natural result of our situation," she hurried on. "We've been a man and woman alone together for several days under intimate conditions that have put us outside the normal conventions of society. But it isn't just sexual attraction, Reilly. I'm in love with you. I'm telling you now, and whenever we do get back to civilization, I'll tell you again. Nothing is going to change the way I feel."

He capped the canteen and straightened. "We're leaving in the morning," he announced unemotionally.

Leah's head recoiled at his unexpected response. "I . . . I thought we were going to wait another day or two until . . . until—"

"—you were stronger," Reilly finished the sentence for her, not sparing a glance in her direction. "Before I got back to camp, I decided there wasn't any point in delaying longer. I think you've recovered enough to travel. If necessary, I'll carry you out."

"Haven't—" she shook her sunstreaked hair helplessly, "haven't you heard anything I said?"

His eyes hardened on her with cycnical amusement. "What do you expect me to reply to it?"

What had she expected? In white-hot humiliation, she didn't know. She hadn't thought he would suddenly admit that he might care for her, too. But his crushing indiffence to her declaration of love sliced deeply with agonizing pain. The only thing that she knew was that she wanted to hurt him back.

Her hand swung in a lightning arc, her open palm striking his lean cheek with stinging force. The attacking hand was captured by punishing fingers that twisted her arm backward until Leah thought it would break. His expression had darkened with savage rage.

"You're hurting me!" she cried out, frightened by the temper she had aroused.

"Am I?" His lip curled in satisfaction.

The fingers shifted their pressure without easing the excruciating pain. The action forced Leah against him, her hips pressed against his muscled thighs while his other hand brutally wound her hair around his fingers and pulled her head back.

Leah tried to struggle, but at her first attempt Reilly twisted her arm farther, checking her protest before it started. As her lips parted to moan her pain, he ruthlessly covered them with his own, grinding them against her teeth until the taste of her own blood was on her tongue.

Tearing his fingers free of her hair, he tugged at her blouse front. Dominated by his devouring mouth and the cruel twisting of her arm, Leah was helpless. The buttons that resisted his fingers were torn off.

Although she was terrified by his assault, it was having a devasting affect on her senses. When his hand closed roughly over her breast, Leah's free hand slid inside his shirt to feel the pagan drumbeat of his heart.

Mercilessly Reilly thrust her away, his green eyes glaring at her contemptuously even as his bared chest rose and fell in disturbed breathing.

"It won't work," he taunted harshly. "I won't be tricked into raping you!"

"I—" Tears swam in her eyes. There was nothing she could say. His accusation wasn't true, not the way he meant it.

The numbed nerves in the arm Reilly had twisted screamed to life when she tried to cover her semi-nakedness. With one hand she tried to button her blouse, but most of the buttons were gone.

A hissing release of breath came from Reilly. "Your clothes are ruined. You'll have to wear one of my shirts." Fingers savagely raked the virile thickness of his black hair as he walked impatiently to get the shirt she had worn earlier as a robe. Avoiding direct contact with her tear-filled gaze, he tossed it to her. "I'll start dinner."

An ominous silence descended on the camp. Later, with shoulders hunched to defend her inner anguish, Leah ate the tasteless food. Her hurt anger kept her from making any attempt to break the silence. It was not the uneasy silence between two strangers, but rather it held the tense hostility of two enemies.

When the scarlet sunset gave way to the purpling night, she crawled into the stiff blanket. She didn't ask Reilly if he would be having an early night before facing tomorrow's walk. She knew without being told that she wouldn't sleep in his arms that night.

Tears washed her face as she turned her back on the fire and Reilly. Even though her pride was severely wounded, she knew nothing had changed. She still loved him as deeply as ever. Nothing would change that.

The swan-dive of a falling star arced across the heavens. Leah watched it until the crystal brightness of a tear got in the way. She pulled the blanket tighter around her shoulders, but the chill was from the inside.

CHAPTER NINE

Leah's knuckles whitened around the end of the lean-to pole, now a walking stick. There was a poignant tightness in her throat as she gazed for the last time at the mock oasis where she had admitted her love for Reilly.

Dawn's early light had lengthened the shadows over the pool, making it look dark and mysterious. It was almost as if the doors were closing on paradise.

The campfire was drowned and the ashes scattered. Soon the desert wind would wipe away any trace of their presence and the waterhole would again belong to the wildlife of the Great Basin.

"Let's go," Reilly said flatly, adjusting with a shrug of his shoulders the pack strapped to his back.

Forcibly turning herself away from the scene, Leah nodded in agreement. She didn't look at him—she avoided it whenever she could. The voltage in his green eyes invariably jolted her with its aloofness.

Reilly probably felt none of the sadness she did about leaving this place where, for a short time, they had been so close in body and spirit. Her family was waiting at the end of their walk, whenever that would be, but Leah knew that if she had been given a choice, she would have stayed here with Reilly. Admittedly, it was a romantic fantasy that was neither logical nor practical.

But she loved him. Oh, God, how she loved him, she thought dispiritedly.

As before, Reilly led the way. The pace was slower than the last time. She knew it was done to conserve her strength. There wasn't any pack on her back this time. Everything they had with them, Reilly carried.

The first few hours of walking, each one punctuated by ten-minute rest stops, Leah felt quite good, not tiring as quickly as she thought she might. Then the sun neared its zenith and the heat began prickling her back.

Reilly set up a noon camp in the middle of the desert valley along the rutted dirt road they had been following for the last several miles. Leah tumbled exhaustedly beneath the lean-to he had immediately erected, swallowed a mouthful of water and closed her eyes.

The nap helped a little. Before they started out again, Reilly inquired distantly as to how she felt. Leah shrugged aside his indifferent question with a stiff, "I'm fine."

For a while she was, but her energy dissipated sooner than it had this morning. Each step seemed to jar her teeth. The ten-minute rest stops seemed to get shorter. She could feel the encroaching weakness, but she gritted her teeth and pushed on.

Reilly stayed close beside her, never more than a few paces ahead. The freshness of his stride goaded Leah to keep walking, reminding her that she was holding him back. If she wasn't along, he would be miles farther than they were now. Bitterly she knew how determined Reilly was that they should find help. He didn't want to spend an hour more than he had to with her.

Turning an ankle on a rock, Leah stumbled and fell to her knees. His hand was under her arm to help her to her feet. She wrenched it away from his hold.

"I can make it," she insisted sharply, and pushed herself upright. Sand had bit into her palms. She rubbed it off on to her slacks.

"Did you twist your ankle?" Reilly studied her quietly with his remote gaze.

Gingerly Leah tested it. It supported her with only a twinge of protest. "It's fine," she answered woodenly. "Let's go."

Reilly handed her the stick she had dropped and started out.

Just before sunset, they stopped for the night. Leah collapsed on to the rutted track, wearily resting her head on her drawn-up knees. Reilly pushed the canteen into her hand and slipped out of his pack. Her hands were shaking too badly from exhaustion to carry the canteen to her mouth without spilling the contents. Finally Reilly had to hold the canteen to her lips.

From the backpack, he handed her a stick of jerky. "We don't have enough water to fix one of the packaged meals."

"I'm not hungry," she waved it aside.

"Eat it," he ordered.

"I'm too tired," Leah grumbled, but she reluctantly took it from him.

"I'm going to see if I can find something for a fire."

Tiredly she chewed on the jerky, finishing it before Reilly returned. She stretched out on the hard, uneven ground, not opening her eyes when she heard his footsteps. He threw the blanket over her, but Leah was certain her aching muscles wouldn't notice the night cold. She heard Reilly starting a fire and guessed he had found fuel of some sort. Then a horrible burning stench filled her nose.

"Whew! What's that?" she rolled over, wrinkling her nose, as she glanced at Reilly.

"There wasn't any wood, but I found some cowchips. They smell, but they burn and we need the fire to keep warm."

Leah pulled the blanket over her head to try to shut out the odorous smoke. Eventually she was simply too tired to care. She didn't even remember the sun sinking below the horizon.

A hand gripped her shoulder. Leah reluctantly opened her eyes, her vision blurring from heavy sleep. A pair of boots were near her head, topped by the narrowed flare of the dusty levis. Her gaze followed the snugly fitting denim material upward over muscular thighs, slim hips and waist to wide shoulders, finally stopping as she met a pair of green eyes.

"It can't be morning," she mumbled, but the sky was light.

"Come on, get up," Reilly said firmly, but he didn't offer to help.

Every muscle, sinew, and nerve in her legs was cramped with stiffness. Reilly, she noticed, was beginning to show signs of fatigue, too, but there was small comfort in that.

Within a few minutes the pack was on his back and they started out again. Her stiff muscles didn't loosen, each step making her wince. Leah relied more heavily on the walking stick to keep her upright when her legs wanted to buckle.

At the second rest stop, she was afraid to sit down for fear she couldn't get up. She leaned heavily on the stick, exhausted nearly beyond the point of endurance.

"How—much farther?" It took an unbelievable amount of effort to even speak.

Reilly's hands were under her arms lowering her to the ground. "I don't know."

"I don't think I can get up," Leah protested, but she was already seated. Of its own accord, her body stretched itself out on the hard ground, her muscles quivering with fatigue.

"You're doing fine," he replied.

'Am I?'' Her laugh was choked off by a lack of breath.

Her lashes fluttered wearily. When she opened them, Reilly was crouching beside her, offering her a lit cigarette to her lips.

''It's the last one,'' he smiled faintly, a mere twist of his mouth. ''We'll have to share.''

He kept a hold of it as she took a long drag on the filtered end. Which was just as well, because Leah doubted she could have held on to it herself.

''I—feel like a dying man having his last cigarette,'' she said, exhaling the smoke in a tired sigh.

''Don't talk. Rest.'' He offered her another puff of the cigarette.

Strange, Leah thought as she felt his fingertips brush her lips, we've said more to each other in these few minutes than we did all day yesterday. Were they both too tired to be angry any more?

After the cigarette was ground into the sand beneath his boot, Reilly lifted Leah to her feet. She couldn't prevent herself from leaning weakly against him. He stiffened away from her, supporting her with his hands and not his body. She knew that not all the barriers had crumbled between them. The walking stick was shoved into her hand and she shifted her weight to it.

They set out at an ambling pace, yet each dragging step was an effort for Leah. Her lungs were bursting with exhaustion, making each breath a sob of determination that pushed her on.

Reilly stopped ahead of her. "Look!" His voice held an undertone of excitement.

Leah paused beside him, forcing her eyes to focus on the direction of his gaze. Flat, sage-covered land stretched endlessly in front of her eyes, the mountain corridor widening to make it larger.

"Where?" she asked hoarsely, seeing nothing to give them hope.

"Off to the right, near the foot of the mountains, there are some buildings. Ranch buildings if I'm not mistaken." His gaze was riveted on the distant point.

All she could make out was some dark squares. She marvelled that he had noticed them at all. Reilly adjusted the shoulder-straps of his makeshift pack and sliced a glance at Leah.

"Let's go."

Their course altered to angle across the open country toward the buildings. For a while, the knowledge that help might be found at those buildings gave Leah a fresh spurt of energy, but too soon it was spent, taking with it what remained of her strength and co-ordination. Her legs became like soft rubber. Without warning they collapsed beneath her and not even the stick could hold her up.

In a haze of total exhaustion, Leah felt Reilly's hands slip under her arms to try to lift her leaden weight.

"It's no use," she breathed. "I can't make it any farther."

"Yes, you can." His voice rang harshly in her ears.

He pulled her to her feet, drawing her arm across

his shoulders and around his neck, while his other arm supported her waist. Half carrying and half dragging Leah, he started forward. She tried to make herself walk to help him. but her tired legs wouldn't obey.

The next thing she knew Reilly was swinging her into his arms. Her head lolled against his shoulder. She felt like a limp rag doll without a solid bone in her body, her head swimming in a mindless state of exhaustion. Distantly, Leah could sense the strain of his rippling muscles to carry her dead weight.

"Leave me, Reilly," she pleaded.

"I'm not leaving you," he refused unconditionally.

Waves of tiredness washed over her and she hadn't the strength to protest any more. She let herself drift away, semi-aware of the arms that held her and the walking motion that carried her across the ground.

The angry bark of a dog finally dragged her eyes open. Her head stirred against his shoulder, turning slightly so she could see ahead of them. Reilly's steps had slowed because of the large dog planted squarely in their path. Beyond him was a dusty white house with curtains at the windows and a wash hanging on the clothesline in the yard.

The screen door on the porch slammed. "Laddie! Come here!" a woman called and the dog stopped barking and retreated to the porch steps. The woman stepped out of the shadows. shielding her eyes against the sun. A small child clung to her legs. "Who are you?" Her voice was friendly but vaguely unsure.

Reilly stopped several feet short of the porch and

the dog. "Our plane crashed eleven days ago in the mountains," he explained calmly. "My woman needs water and a place to rest. May we come in?"

"Yes, yes, of course!" the woman exclaimed. She clapped her hands at the dog. "Laddie, go and lie down. We were notified of the search, my husband and I, but we had no idea the plane had gone down anywhere near here. Come in, come in."

Leah didn't hear half of what the woman said. Her heart was still singing from Reilly's words, 'my woman.' Her hazel eyes lovingly searched his face, dusty and lined with weariness yet indomitably strong. Had he meant that? Or was it only a figure of speech?

"Are you hurt?" the woman rushed holding the screen door open for Reilly, a wide-eyed little girl still clinging to her legs. "Shall I call a doctor? Or an ambulance?"

"No, it's just exhaustion from a long walk." Reilly stopped inside the door. "Where can she rest?"

"There's a sofa in the living room. This way." The woman ushered them into the living room, hovering uncertainly for a minute. "I'll get some water." She walked swiftly out of the room, the little girl hurrying in her shadow.

Gently Reilly lowered Leah on to the sofa, plumping pillows beneath her head. "Comfortable?"

She nodded, smiling wanly. "I didn't remember anything could be so soft. Reilly—" She didn't finish the sentence as the woman returned carrying a pitcher of water and glasses on a tray.

Leah drank thirstily from the glass Reilly held to her lips, then sank back against the pillows as some of the strength ebbed back into her weary limbs.

The woman disentangled the little girl from her legs, bending slightly toward her. "Go out to the barn, Mary, and get your father. Tell him to hurry." She turned to Reilly, who was pouring a glass of water for himself. "Is there anything else I can get for you? Whisky? Food?"

"Black coffee, if you have some." He straightened away from the sofa. "And would you show me where the telephone is so I can notify the authorities?"

The little girl named Mary had shyly inched past Reilly, then dashed out of the room, the screen door banging as she ran for her father.

"The telephone is in the kitchen, and I do have some coffee on," the woman smiled.

Reilly glanced down at Leah lying on the couch. "You'll be okay. I'll only be gone a few minutes."

"I'm fine," she assured him softly, warmed by the flecks of concern that had been present in his green eyes.

As Reilly and the woman left the room, Leah relaxed against the cushions and pillows. It seemed strange to have four walls surrounding her and a ceiling instead of the open sky above her head. Tonight she'd be taking a hot bath, changing into clean clothes, and sleeping in a soft bed. She'd willingly trade it all—

The light, quick footsteps belonging to the woman entered the living room. "Here's your coffee. It's hot

and black and sweet, the way your husband ordered it.
He said to drink it all," she smiled brightly, her plain
features, freckled by the desert sun, suddenly taking
on a rare beauty.

Leah pushed herself into a sitting position, using
the pillows to help prop herself up. A hint of pink
brought color to her cheeks as she held the mug of
coffee with both hands.

"Reilly isn't my . . . husband." Much as she wished
she could say otherwise.

The woman looked surprised. "I thought . . . that
is . . . " She laughed to cover her confusion. "I guess I
just presumed you were married without thinking.
I'm sorry."

"There's no need to apologize," Leah insisted,
carefully sipping the hot coffee, some of her weakness
easing as the sweet liquid traveled down her throat.

"I'm Tina Edwards," the woman introduced
herself.

"Leah Talbot," supplied Leah.

"This must have been quite an ordeal for you."

Ordeal. How could she explain to the woman that it
hadn't been an ordeal? Despite the shock of the crash,
the days she had been delirious with fever from her
infected wound, Leah couldn't think of the time she
had been alone with Reilly as an ordeal. It had been
primitively idyllic.

"It wasn't really too bad," she answered, choosing
her words carefully. "The worst was today and
yesterday." When Reilly had withdrawn from her,
she added to herself.

"I can imagine," the woman nodded understandingly "Walking in this heat even a short distance can be exhausting."

The screen door slammed and the little girl came racing into the living room to stand beside her mother, peering at Leah through her lashes. There were other footsteps. Then the sound of a strange man's voice speaking to Reilly

"That's my husband, Mike He was doctoring one of the horses in the barn." the woman explained.

Leah swallowed more coffee, the sugar and the caffeine stimulating her senses. She glanced up when Reilly entered the living room, accompanied by a shorter man wearing a straw cowboy hat and sunglasses. Intense weariness was etched around Reilly's eyes and mouth. She marvelled that he could still keep pushing himself on

"Mr Edwards has offered to drive us into Tonopah." said Reilly, the same tiredness in his face lacing his voice. "Your family will be there to meet us They're being notified that you are safe and well."

"Are we leaving now?" she asked.

"As soon as you finish your coffee."

Concealing a sigh of regret, Leah carried the mug to her lips. She had hoped for some time alone with Reilly, but he seemed to be avoiding any opportunity for a private discussion between them. There was little reason for her to object to his plans. Later, some time, she would speak to him and she wouldn't allow him to stop her She swallowed the last of the coffee.

"I'm ready." she said. When Reilly bent to lift her

into his arms, she shook her head. "I'm a little wobbly, but I think I can walk."

His fingers closed over her elbow to help her to her feet. She swayed unsteadily for a moment, then found her balance. But Reilly didn't release his grip on her arm, his touch impersonal and cool, as he guided her toward the door.

"Thank you, Mrs. Edwards," Leah smiled when they paused near the screen door, "for everything."

There was a brief exchange of goodbyes before they went out to the car. Leah sat alone in the back seat, so she could strech out and rest, Reilly had said. She was still tired and she did rest, but her thoughts kept straying to the man seated in front of her. Although she tried, she couldn't concentrate on the welcome she would receive when they arrived.

Several miles from the house, the ranch road joined a secondary road that led them to the highway. Mike Edwards' foot was heavy on the accelerator and the utility poles whizzed by the car window in a blur. Yet it was more than an hour before they reached the outskirts of Tonopah, Nevada.

They stopped in front of the building housing the sheriff's office. Leah straightened stiffly in her seat, wincing at the soreness of her muscles. Her fingers closed over the door handle, but Reilly was already out of the car, opening the door for her. His hand firmly gripped her elbow to help her out and steady her once she was standing on the sidewalk. She resisted when he tried to lead her toward the building.

When his cool jade eyes glanced questioningly at

her, Leah spoke in a low voice so Mike Edwards couldn't overhear. "Reilly, please, we have to talk."

"About what?" His dark head was tipped to the side, his expression deliberately devoid of understanding.

She swallowed nervously. "About us."

"Leah, I don't see—" Reilly began, with an arrogant kind of patience.

"Leah!" A familiar voice interrupted him with the strident call of her name. "Leah!"

She turned slightly in the direction of the voice, and a smile of growing joy curved her mouth as she recognized the tall and lanky, sandy-haired man half walking and half running toward her.

"Lonnie!" The bubble of happiness made her brother's name a choked sound, so Leah said it again. "Lonnie!"

She took one step toward him. Beyond him she could see the blue Air Force uniform of her father emerging from a car along with vivacious figure of her mother. Then Lonnie's hands were on her waist, lifting her into the air and hugging her tightly as he swung her around.

"You're all right. You're all right!" her brother kept repeating as if to convince himself while he buried his head in her sunstreaked hair.

"Yes," Leah whispered with sobbing happiness. "Yes, I'm all right."

He finally let her feet touch the ground, and drew his head back to look at her, unmanly tears shimmering in his brown eyes. "You crazy little nut!"

Every word reinforced the closeness of the bond between them. "What did you think you were doing?"

Tears flowed down her cheeks. "I was coming to see you—to surprise you for your birthday."

"Leah, my baby!" At the tearfully happy voice of her mother, Lonnie released her from his embrace letting her turn to meet both their parents.

Leah was immediately engulfed in another tight embrace, her arms winding themselves around their mother and feeling the shudders of relief and happiness that coursed through her.

"My baby, my darling," her mother whispered over and over. "We've been so worried. They'd given you up for dead. We

"I'm all right, Momma. She slid one arm around her father's waist as he stood erectly beside them unable to express his relief and joy. She hugged them both lightly. Her father's hand tentatively stroked her hair as she buried her face against the buttons of his uniform.

"You gave us quite a scare, child," he said tightly.

"I know, Daddy." Leah whispered. She tossed back her head and gazed into his face, seeing the love shining in his eyes that he couldn't express in words.

"Heavens, just look at you!" Her mother brushed the tears from her face. then shakily tried to do the same for Leah. "You're a sight, Leah Talbot! Your clothes are a mess. You must have lost ten pounds and you look as brown as an Indian."

Leah stiffened away from her parents, glancing

frantically over her shoulder. Reilly wasn't standing beside the car where she had left him. Her heart leapt in fear. Then she saw him nearly at the building's entrance.

"Reilly!" She pulled the rest of the way free of her parents' arms, ignoring their confused frowns. Taking a quick step to follow him, she called again. "Reilly!"

She could see the tensing of his wide shoulders as he hesitated, then stopped. He pivoted back abruptly, impatience underlining his reluctance. She knew he had hoped to slip away unnoticed during the reunion with her parents.

"Reilly, don't leave—" Her voice lilted upward as she nearly tacked on 'me.' She tried to cover her lack of pride with, "I want you to meet my family."

His long strides covered the distance that separated them with an eagerness that said he wanted to get this over and be on his way. His implacable features could have been carved out of hard granite, an emotionless statue with impassive jewelled eyes of jade. He looked noble and proud, without feeling.

Leah was almost afraid that if she touched him, she too would turn to stone. Quickly she introduced him to her parents, her heart freezing at the distantly polite smile he gave them.

"This is Reilly Smith. We shared the charter of the plane," she explained tautly, feeling nervous and awkward. "I wouldn't be here if it wasn't for him." Her voice sounded brittle with its forced cheerfulness.

There was a brief exchange of courteous responses to the introductions. Then Reilly took a withdrawing step backwards. "It was a pleasure meeting all of you," he said politely. "If you'll excuse me now. I have some things to attend to, and I know you'd like to be with your daughter."

As he started to turn away, Leah caught at his arm. "Where are you going?"

Reilly glanced at her hand on his arm, then blandly into her upturned face. "To the sheriff's office to give him an account of the plane crash."

"I should go with you." She didn't want to let him out of her sight. If she did, she was afraid she would never see him again.

"I'm certain I can answer any questions myself." he refused firmly. "If the sheriff needs to corroborate my story, he can talk to you after you've had some time to rest. Right now you're exhausted, too tired to think straight and know what you're saying."

Leah knew what he was implying—that she only imagined she was in love with him. Her teeth bit tightly into her lower lip to hide its tremor.

"I do know," she insisted in a choked murmur. Before he could stop her, she slid her arms around his waist and clung to him. burying her head against his chest to hear the beat of his heart and make certain he wasn't made of stone. In a voice so low that only he could hear, she cast aside her pride. "When will I see you again?"

His hands hesitated on her shoulders for a tanatalizing moment, then slid firmly down to grasp her arms and push her away from him. Her eyes were tear-bright as she met the unrelenting indifference of his.

"Go with your parents, Leah. Get some food and some sleep." His hard mouth moved upward at the corners in what was supposed to be a smile, but it left her chilled. "We'll have dinner some time and laugh about our misadventure."

His cool gaze flicked briefly to her parents, then he released her and left. She watched him striding so easily away from her and felt a pain so intense that she wanted to die. Self-consciously she turned back to her family, glancing first at Lonnie.

Her brother's brown eyes had narrowed on the man's shirt she wore, resting briefly on the thrust of her breasts against the material. The absence of a brassiere was obvious. Quiet speculation was in his eyes when they raised to meet her glance before swinging to look at their father. His calculating gaze was directed at Reilly disappearing into the building.

Leah knew what was going through their minds. They had just realized she had spent eleven days alone with a man. Now they were wondering how she had spent the eleven nights.

Lonnie's arm curved around her shoulders and he hugged her against his side. "Let's take her back to the motel where she can clean up," he smiled at his parents. There was a challenging glint in his eyes when he met his father's gaze. "Then we'll eat, since Leah owes me a belated birthday dinner."

CHAPTER TEN

A hand brushed the hair away from her cheek tucking it behind her ears. then running to rest gently along her cheek.

'Wake up, Leah,'' a male voice coaxed softly.

Her lashes fluttered but didn't open. "Mmmm. Contentedly she rubbed her cheek against the masculine hand. "Have I told you I love you?'' she whispered with a blissful smile.

"Not lately,'' was the mocking reply.

"I love you, Reilly Smith '' Her voice vibrated huskily with the depth of her emotion.

The hand was instantly withdrawn. "Wake up Leah! You're dreaming.'' the voice ordered tightly

With a start her eyes flashed open. Bewilderedly Leah realized that she wasn't sleeping in Reilly's arms. She was in a bed, with a pillow instead of his shoulder beneath her head. And her brother Lonnie was standing beside the bed, his hands shoved deep in the pockets of his trousers, a troubled frown drawing his eyebrows together.

Hot color flamed through her face as she realized she had mistaken her brother for Reilly and guessed the conclusion he must have jumped to at her words. She rolled on to her back, turning her head toward the window and the heavy drapes that had been drawn to shut out the sunlight.

"Is it time for dinner already?" Leah blinked, as if unware of what she had revealed.

"Dinner?" His laugh, instead of being lightly teasing, had overtones of bitterness. "You've been asleep for nearly thirty-six hours."

"I have?" Her head jerked toward him in disbelief.

Leah started to sit up, then rememberd she wasn't wearing anything and quickly drew the covers up under her arms before shifting into a half-sitting position. It seemed only a few hours ago that her mother had suggested she take a nap after her bath.

"Mom was going out to buy some clothes to wear." She nervously ran her fingers through her hair.

"They're over on the chair." He nodded his head abruptly toward the chair. "I'll go next door to the folks' room while you get dressed." Lonnie paused at the door, his hand on the knob. "Leah—" He seemed to hesitate.

"Yes?" She held her breath.

"Never mind," he sighed with an impatient shake of his head. "I'll meet you over there."

Afterward, Leah wished Lonnie had asked the question that had been uppermost in his mind. It would have eased the strange tension that suddenly sprang between them. She tried to be bright and cheerful, the way her parents expected her to be, when they breakfasted together later, but she kept lapsing into moody silences, her thoughts wandering to Reilly—where he was—what he was doing—when or if she would see him.

Partly the cause was due to the subject of their conversation which continued when they returned to her parents' room. Her parents were naturally interested in recieving a first-hand account of what had happened when the plane crashed and what she had done during the eleven days she was missing.

Naturally Leah couldn't relate the story without explaining the large part Reilly had played in her survival. The more often she repeated his name, the more often she thought about him. She had only to close her eyes to see him in her mind and remember what it was like to be in his arms.

"Maybe we should take you to see a doctor this afternoon," her father suggested.

"What for?" Leah flashed defensively, then flushed guiltily at the grim look from her brother.

Her father frowned, his eyes narrowing. "To verify that the gash on your arm is healing properly and make certain there are no signs of infection."

Too late Leah remembered only moments before telling them of the time she had been ill with fever

Absently she touched the small bandage on her left arm.

'It's fine. There's no need to see a doctor,'' she murmured self-consciously. She moved away from the motel room window.

'Really, dear,'' her mother laughed, unaware of the tension that had enveloped her daughter. "I can't help marvelling at the way you avoided catching pneumonia, considering how cold it gets in this part of the country at night.''

Leah flinched. Her mother had not meant it as a subtle probe into the relationship between Leah and Reilly. But Leah knew she had been carefully sidestepping any comment that might reveal what she felt. She had basically never kept anything from her family before, and her lack of openness was making her feel guilty when there was no reason.

'Actually, Mom, it was quite simple.'' She lifted her chin in an unconsciously defiant pose. ''Reilly and I slept together to keep warm.'' A pregnant silence followed her statement. ''I didn't mean that the way it sounded,'' she inserted, nervously reaching for the pack of cigarettes sitting on the dresser. ''Reilly didn't actually make love to me if that's what you're wondering.''

''Leah '' her mother hesitated, searching for the right words, ''we honestly weren't thinking anything like that.''

'I know, but '' Leah pressed her lips tightly together and quickly lit a cigarette.

"But '' her father picked up the unfinished part of

Leah's sentence, his hands clasped behind his back as he stared out the window, "it's what you were thinking."

Leah stared at the glowing tip of the cigarette. "I'm in love with him, Dad."

"I see. And how does Mr. Smith feel about you?"

She crushed the unsmoked cigarette out in the ashtray. "I don't know. He—" she glanced at her father, "he hasn't called, has he?"

"No," her father answered.

"Leah, are you quite sure you know what you're saying?" her mother asked gently. "Maybe the emotion you feel is only gratitude. Patients often fall in love with their doctor."

"No." Leah's sunstreaked hair swung about her shoulders as she shook her head and laughed without humor. "It definitely isn't gratitude."

Her father turned away from the window, his gaze piercingly intent. "You barely know the man, Leah," he snapped impatiently.

"I can't accept that argument, Dad," she replied calmly. "I spent eleven days alone with him on the desert under conditions that would bring out the true colors of any man."

It was becoming painful to talk about Reilly. Leah didn't know how long her shell of composure would last before it cracked and all the uncertainties of whether he loved her or would love her would come tumbling out.

She nervously smoothed a hand over the waist of

the lightweight cotton dress. "If you don't mind, I think I'll go to my room and freshen up."

She wasn't surprised when her parents didn't attempt to detain her. She guessed they wanted to discuss the situation in private. Naturally they were dubious that their daughter had fallen in love with a man who was a complete stranger to them.

In her own room, Leah leaned against the door she had just closed and tried to take her own stock of the situation. Her thoughts were immediately interrupted by a knock on the door.

"Who is it?" she asked impatiently, wanting to be alone.

"It's me—Lonnie. Can I come in?"

"Of course." With a sigh, she shot back the bolt on the door and opened it. His eyes flicked thoughtfully to her tense expression as he wandered into the room.

"What did you want?" Leah asked with forced nonchalance.

"My company gave me leave of absence while you were missing. Now that you've been found, I'll be reporting back to work in the morning," her brother answered idly. "Dad's made arrangements for the three of you to fly back to Vegas tomorrow. He's going on alone to Alaska from there and Mom will join him in a couple of weeks."

Leah waited without commenting on the news. Her brother was leading up to something, but she didn't know what.

"That was quite a write-up in the paper about your

Reilly Smith," Lonnie went on in the same casual tone. "He's quite well known in his field."

"He's not my Reilly Smith." She stared at the hands she had clasped in front of her, fingers twisting nervously.

"But you do want him to be?" Lonnie asked quietly for verification of her love.

"I love him, Lonnie, more than I ever thought it was possible to love a man," Leah answered, then laughed bitterly. "For all the good it does me."

"Why do you say that?" He tipped his head to the side, a wayward lock of sandy brown hair falling across his forehead.

"Because he said nearly the same thing Mom and Dad just said, only in a different way." She walked agitatedly to the dresser mirror, pausing to gaze at her brother's watchful reflection. "He said that the time we spent together would seem like a dream that never really happened, once we got back. He meant that I would forget him when I was surrounded by the civilized world again."

"But you haven't," Lonnie supplied.

"No." She turned away from the mirror. "Lonnie, do you know where he's staying?"

"You want to go see him, is that it?" He smiled understandingly as she nodded her affirmative answer. "I don't know, but it shouldn't be too hard to find out in a town the size of Tonopah. Let me make a few phone calls."

When he located the motel where Reilly was registered, Leah asked him to take her there. If Reilly wouldn't make the effort to see her, then she would make one last effort to see him before she resigned herself to the fact that he didn't care about her.

"You don't need to come in with me, Lonnie," she said when he got out of the car to walk with her to the motel entrance.

"He wasn't in when I called. He might not be in yet I'll go in with you to see." her brother smiled, linking her arms in his.

"If Reilly isn't in. I'm going to wait until he comes." Her chin lifted with determination. "I won't leave without seeing him."

Inside the motel, Lonnie asked her to wait for him at the entrance door while he checked at the desk. A few minutes later he was back

"Come on." His hand gripped her elbow as he guided her past a row of rooms.

"Is he in?" she asked anxiously.

"No." He dangled a key in the air. "But you can wait for him in his room."

"How did you get that?"

'I greased the right palm." Lonnie grinned cheekily. "I couldn't have my sister waiting in a motel lobby for a man." He squeezed her hand when tears misted her eyes, the tight lump in her throat making it impossible for her to voice her gratitude. His gaze shifted to the numbered doors. "Here's his room." He unlocked the door and opened it for her. "Good luck. Sis, and if he doesn't listen to you, call me and I'll talk to him."

"What would I ever do without you?" Leah murmured, hugging him tightly.

"You could make it without me." His voice was muffled against her hair as he gave the top of her head an affectionate kiss. "But if you love this guy as much as you say you do, I don't think you could make it without him. So fight for him, Leah, with everything you have."

"I will," she promised.

Then she was alone in the motel room and Lonnie's footsteps were receding.

There wasn't a clock in the room, so she had no idea how long she waited for Reilly to return. It seemed like hours and hours that she wandered aimlessly from the bed to the lone chair to the window and back to the bed. She thought of countless arguments she could make and rehearsed them over and over again.

When she heard a key inserted in the lock, Leah forgot them all. She stood frozen beside the chair as the door opened and Reilly walked in. He didn't see her immediately as he shut the door and tossed a jacket on the bed, so she had a few precious seconds to take in his tiredly drawn features.

His sunbrowned fingers had just impatiently unbuttoned the top buttons of his shirt when he saw her. He stopped shortly, his green eyes narrowing into jade slits. Leah hoped to surprise him, possibly make him reveal some small sign of gladness at seeing her again. She was disappointed.

"What are you doing here, Leah?" His mouth thinned grimly.

Her throat went dry. It all suddenly seemed hopeless. "I came to see you. I wanted to talk." She moistened her dry lips. "I've been waiting for you for hours. Where have you been?"

"I had to show the sheriff the location of the crash," Reilly breathed in deeply. "I stayed around until they uncovered Grady's body from the wreckage, then came back to make the arrangements with his family to have the body sent back to Las Vegas for burial. I imagine one of the sheriff's men will be taking your luggage to your motel."

Although she spared a silent thought of sympathy for Grady's family and a flash of grief at his death, Leah knew she didn't dare let Reilly sidetrack her from the reason she had come.

"You could have brought my things to the motel," she said. "Why didn't you?"

He rubbed a hand tiredly over his jaw and chin. "Because I didn't want to see you," Reilly answered with brutal honesty. "Look, I'm hot and tired. I need a shower and some sleep. So why don't you say whatever it is you've come here to say and get out!"

Leah flinched. "I love you, Reilly."

"Dammit, Leah, we've been over that before!" he growled angrily beneath his breath.

"And you believed that once I was back with my family and the so-called real world, what I felt for you would fade like the memory of a dream." The corners of her mouth lifted in a sad smile. "Look around you, Reilly. There are man-made walls and ceilings, beds and chairs and running hot and cold water. Outside there's concrete instead of sage-dotted desert sand and cars and trucks instead of jackrabbits and snake. But I'm still me and you are still you. And I still love you, more than I did before, because I found out how empty I feel not waking up in your arms."

A tense silence enclosed them. His level gaze crossed the width of the room to hold hers. His impassive face, austerely handsome, was a granite mask carved by the sun and desert wind. Abruptly he pivoted away, an impatient stride carrying him to the dresser table.

"You don't know what you're saying," Reilly muttered. Ice from a styrofoam container clunked into a plastic glass, joined by the melted water in the container.

Leah reached behind her and unzipped her dress. "I told you once that if you left me, I would follow." She slipped her arms out of the sleeves. "I meant that, Reilly. If you don't want me as your wife, then I'll stay with you as your woman." She stepped out of the dress as it slid to the floor.

"Will you—" Reilly turned toward her. His eyes flashed over her semi-naked state. Whatever he was going to say was never finished. "What the hell are you doing!" The plastic glass was shoved on to the table, water sloshing over the sides. In lightning strides, he eliminated the distance between them, tearing the bedspread from the bed and throwing it around her.

Calmly Leah met his fiery gaze. "A naked body is part of nature," she repeated the words he had once used. "You've seen me once. Why should I be ashamed for you to see me unclothed again?"

"The circumstances are different," Reilly snapped, drawing the spread tightly around her like a cocoon.

"How are they different?" she challenged, swaying toward him, her lips parting in a deliberate invitation.

His fingers dug into the soft flesh of her upper arm, preventing her from leaning against his chest yet not allowing her to move away. His gaze was riveted on the shimmering moistness of her lips, his breathing suddenly not as controlled and even as it had been.

"Because I'm thinking like a white man and not an Indian," he answered with raw huskiness.

"And you want me," Leah whispered the definition of his statement.

Hungrily his mouth devoured hers, crushing her against the hard length of his body so that she might know how desperately he wanted her. His hands roamed possessively over her, fighting the folds of the bedspread that he had wrapped her so tightly in, but he didn't let her work free of its protective covering. Leah's appetite had to be satified with returning his passionate kiss.

Reilly dragged his mouth from hers, his hunger unsatisfied but controlled for the moment as the iron band of his arms held her a willing prisoner.

"You need more time, Leah." His husky voice breathed against her sunstreaked hair.

"Time won't change how much I love you or how much I want you," she protested achingly.

"How can I make you understand?" Reilly

groaned, his mouth moving over her forehead and eyes. "If I make you mine, Leah, I could never let you go. I love you so much that I'd make you stay with me whether you wanted to or not. I know you believe you care for me."

'Oh, Reilly darling!" A searing happiness brought a breathless laugh from her throat. "I'm not a patient falling in love with her doctor. I'm a woman in love with a man, and I don't ever want you to let me go." The iron band of his arms constricted. "If you do love me, why didn't you want to see me?" she asked tightly, still trying to believe that Reilly was telling her the truth.

'Because I knew if I kept seeing you, without giving you time to consider your feelings, I wouldn't be able to keep myself from making love to you. You have no idea what torture it is not to possess you when I love you so completely." Reilly unlocked his arms and held her face his eyes gazing into it and reflecting it 'Please, put your dress on." he murmured huskily so we can go talk to your parents about our wedding."

Diamond tears misted rainbow-bright on her lashes. "You do want to marry me!" she breathed, her heart swelling with unmeasurable bliss.

Reilly looked deeply into her eyes. "You'll be my wife, then I'll make you my woman." His dark head bent toward hers and she lifted her mouth for his kiss.

Have you missed any of these best-selling Harlequin Romances?

By popular demand... to help complete your collection of Harlequin Romances

48 titles listed on the following pages...

Harlequin Reissues

Harlequin Reissues

Complete and mail this coupon today!

Harlequin Reader Service
MPO Box 707
Niagara Falls, N.Y. 14302

In Canada:
649 Ontario St.
Stratford, Ont. N5A 6W2

Please send me the following Harlequin Romances. I am enclosing my check or money order for 95¢ for each novel ordered, plus 25¢ to cover postage and handling.

☐ 1282	☐ 1394	☐ 1481
☐ 1284		☐ 1483
☐ 1285	☐ 1433	☐ 1484
☐ 1288	☐ 1435	☐ 1638
☐ 1289	☐ 1439	☐ 1643
☐ 1292	☐ 1440	☐ 1647
☐ 1293	☐ 1444	☐ 1651
☐ 1294	☐ 1449	☐ 1652
☐ 1295	☐ 1456	☐ 1654
☐ 1353	☐ 1457	☐ 1659
☐ 1363		☐ 1675
☐ 1365	☐ 1464	☐ 1677
☐ 1368	☐ 1468	☐ 1686
☐ 1371	☐ 1473	☐ 1691
☐ 1372	☐ 1475	☐ 1695
☐ 1384	☐ 1477	☐ 1697
☐ 1390	☐ 1478	

Number of novels checked _____ @ 95¢ each = $_____

N.Y. and N.J. residents add appropriate sales tax $_____

Postage and handling $_____.25

TOTAL $_____

NAME _____
(Please print)

ADDRESS _____

CITY _____

STATE/PROV. _____ ZIP/POSTAL CODE _____

PRS 231

YOU'LL L♥VE
Harlequin Magazine

for women who enjoy reading fascinating stories of exciting romance in exotic places

SUBSCRIBE NOW!

This is a colorful magazine especially designed and published for the readers of Harlequin novels.

Now you can receive your very own copy delivered right to your home every month throughout the year for only 75¢ an issue.

This colorful magazine is available only through Harlequin Reader Service, so enter your subscription now!

In every issue...

Here's what you'll find:

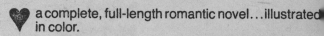

♥ a complete, full-length romantic novel...illustrated in color.

♥ exotic travel feature...an adventurous visit to a romantic faraway corner of the world.

♥ delightful recipes from around the world...to bring delectable new ideas to your table.

♥ reader's page...your chance to exchange news and views with other Harlequin readers.

♥ other features on a wide variety of interesting subjects.

Start enjoying your own copies of Harlequin magazine immediately by completing the subscription reservation form.

Not sold in stores!

Harlequin Reader Service   In Canada:
MPO Box 707,   649 Ontario St.
Niagara Falls, N.Y. 14302   Stratford, Ont. N5A 6W2

I wish to subscribe to Harlequin magazine beginning with the next issue. I enclose my check or money order for $9.00 for 12 monthly issues.

NAME_____

ADDRESS_____

CITY_____

STATE/PROV._____ ZIP/POSTAL CODE_____

PRS 231